# Look for More Titles by Cassandra Chandler

LINGERING TOUCH

Other Works
CRAFTING A WRITER'S LIFE: Building a Foundation

*Coming Soon*

*The Blades of Janus*
PERIHELION

*The Department of Homeworld Security*
Nothing to Declare

# Duel Citizenship

The Department of Homeworld
Security
Book Seven

*Cassandra Chandler*

# Copyright Page

This book is pure fiction. All characters, places, names, and events are products of the author's imagination or used solely in a fictitious manner. Any resemblance to any people, places, things, or events that have ever existed or will ever exist is entirely coincidental.

Duel Citizenship
The Department of Homeworld Security, Book Seven
Copyright © 2017 by Cassandra Chandler
Print ISBN: 978-1-945702-38-9
Digital ISBN: 978-1-945702-27-3

First eBook edition: September 2017
First print edition: December 2018
10 9 8 7 6 5 4 3 2 1

cassandra-chandler.com
P.O. Box 91
Mission, Kansas 66201

# Dedication

For all my lizard friends.

*Don't miss out on any of the alien action.*
*Subscribe to Cassandra Chandler's newsletter at*
*cassandra-chandler.com!*

# Chapter One

"This planet's diversity is remarkable." Ari checked the readouts on his screen again. The geological scans were returning data he wasn't sure he was interpreting correctly. "Are we really hovering over a sandbar? That people *live* on?"

Kira smiled. "Earthlings are innovative, especially considering the level of their technology. Perhaps because of it. They're unable to build space stations that can support large numbers of people and don't have the technology to make dome worlds. They have to make do with what they have, and the planet is heavily populated."

"Yet they still leave vast areas untouched." He wished he could see more through the viewports, but the sky was still dark.

"That's a good thing. They're already starting to understand the importance of managing their resources." Her smile faded. "And we need to help them stay on the right path—especially once they find out about us."

"Understood." Ari turned his attention back to his scans with more focus.

Someone was using advanced technology nearby. Technology that rivaled—if not surpassed—that of their own scout ship. Kira kept the vessel steady, hovering high above one of the smaller cities in the region while Ari tried to pinpoint the source.

"I can't get the source of the reading narrowed down to more than a few miles radius," he said. "I think we need to move in closer."

"We only have twenty minutes till the sun rises. I need to be back at headquarters by then."

"I'm detecting a stretch of road near the area of interest that isn't heavily traveled. If you drop me off there, I can investigate further."

"You'll need to set up a base of operations. You'll be here for days and will have to interact with Earthlings."

"Yes, sir."

She didn't respond at first, except to scowl as her brow furrowed. "Are you sure you're up for this? Earth can be… bewildering."

"I've been acclimating for months. All of us have."

And yet it was still strange to see his commanding officer wearing Earth clothing—jeans and a light sweater. Her dark brown hair was in a loose ponytail instead of the regulation bun that was required when she was in uniform. If their scout ship malfunctioned, they needed to be able to blend in with the Earthlings of the area. Their shining silver uniforms would not help with that.

Ari's outfit was designed to match the culture of this region of the continent. They had anticipated the possibility that he would need to scout out the area.

Brendan, Kira's Earthling bondmate, had insisted that Ari wear ridiculous shoes called "loafers". They barely felt like shoes at all, especially compared with the boots he was used to. Apparently, wearing heavier shoes in the warm climate of Florida would make him stand out, even during their early spring season.

As if the shoes weren't bad enough, he was also wearing a brightly colored button-down shirt that was decorated with what was called a "tropical pattern" and pale tan shorts that barely reached his knees.

At least the shorts had plenty of pockets.

He was supposed to look like a tourist so that anyone who noticed he was out of place wouldn't think too hard about him. Brendan had packed a duffle bag with everything Ari should need for his mission. Money, clothing, identification cards.

The watch Ari wore integrated Coalition technology with Earth's in an inconspicuous form—another innovation from Brendan, though with the help of Coalition engineers. In addition to being a communication device, it could act as a small scanner, letting Ari covertly search for the alien technology he was looking for.

He had to admit, the Planetary Liaison had chosen well in pair-bonding with Brendan, even if she had done it for something as irrational as love.

"This isn't going to be like interactions at the mansion," Kira said. "You've been spending time with specific Earthlings in the controlled setting of our headquarters—which is in a radically different ecosystem from this one."

That was true enough. It was hard to believe that they had flown from mountains covered in snow to the sub-tropical setting around them on the same planet. He'd been on worlds with variations in their ecosystems, of course, but planets with diversity as extreme as Earth's were rare.

Once more, he wished they could fly during daylight so that he could see the change in vegetation with his own eyes instead of scanner readouts. Coalition protocol dictated that all in-atmosphere flights had to take place at night, even when their ship was cloaked.

Kira watched him silently, lips pulled in a concerned frown.

"I can handle it, sir," Ari said.

She nodded curtly, maneuvering the ship toward the road he had pointed out, then setting it down in a gentle landing. He released the clamp that kept his chair still and swiveled around to face the back of the small ship.

"The ground will shift beneath your feet," she said.

He paused in unfastening his safety harness. "Excuse me?"

"I read your file. You've spent most of your time aboard ships and stations."

"That's right."

"You're about to step onto a sandbar. When you walk on sand, it moves."

He smiled, trying to reassure her—and himself. "I'll do my best not to fall."

"See that you don't." She was grimacing again, dark eyes narrowed. "This mission—what we're doing here— it's important. We have no idea how many alien species have invaded Earth. If we can't get this under control, the High Council may revoke the preservation status for the planet and bring it into the Coalition."

He nodded. "And Earth isn't ready for that. I understand."

"I'm not sure that you do. But you will, after you spend some time here." She smiled faintly. "Enjoy it while you can."

"Yes, sir."

"Check in every three hours outside of your rest cycle. Dismissed."

He half-crawled out of the chair, keeping his body hunched over as he grabbed his bag. Kira opened the hatch and a ramp slid out from within the ship's hull, which had decloaked to help Ari make his way outside.

He had to turn sideways to exit the ship, bypassing the short ramp and stepping out with one foot on the road while ducking to maneuver the rest of his body through the opening. Most Sadirians were genetically engineered to be small and wiry. Living on dome worlds and space stations, creating citizens who were bigger was considered a waste of resources. Of course, accidents happened—like Ari.

His size had bothered him until he'd been assigned to the *Arbiter*. The first time he'd watched General Serath—the highest ranking military officer in the Coalition's fleet—do the same twisting maneuver to exit a tiny scout ship was the first time Ari had actually felt proud to be a glitch.

He was in good company, at least, especially aboard the *Arbiter*. Most of the crew were glitches. Serath's first officer, Khel, was even bigger than Ari, though not by much.

The *Arbiter* had been the first place that had felt like home.

Being among the team assigned to find and contain the aliens who were trespassing on Earth was a huge show of Serath's trust. Ari still sometimes wished that he had remained with the crew when the ship went back to Sadr-4 to try to convince the High Council to recognize Earth's First Contact committee, though.

Earth had a strange effect on his fellow Sadirians. General Serath had been the first to pair-bond with an Earthling, going so far as to change his name to "Adam Smith", not that Ari had been able to start thinking of him that way yet. *Adam* wore his hair differently, carried himself differently, and seemed to have been fundamentally changed by his experiences on Earth.

As if that wasn't enough, Kira had bonded with Brendan. Sorca with Eric. Moons, even Khel had bonded with Brendan's sister, Paige. And then Vay had fallen for an Earthling named Henry.

The others in their small team were already talking about possibly bonding with an Earthling. Most were excited, after seeing how happy their fellow soldiers were with their chosen partners. And it wasn't just the Sadirians who were bonding.

The Scorpiian that they'd been hunting for months had fallen in love with an Earthling and pair-bonded with her. Ari still couldn't believe the cold-blooded assassin now smiled and laughed—and even went on missions alongside the team. At least, when he wasn't busy playing video games or "spending quality time" with his bondmate.

Zemanni had actually been able to convince the pair of Lyrians living at headquarters that he'd changed. That was a good thing, since the female—Barbara—had been eager to tear him apart *again* when he first showed up.

It was a lot to wrap his head around.

Ari trotted away from the scout vessel as the hatch closed and the ramp retracted. Kira swung the ship around, nodding to him through the main viewport. A rippling wave passed over the ship's hull as it vanished.

He felt a slight turbulence in the air as it took off, heading back for headquarters. She'd be back with her own Earthling bondmate before Ari made it to the town.

Especially if he didn't get moving.

Kira's warning about the shifting sands had unnerved him a bit. The road was solid, at least. He crossed to the edge, using the pre-dawn light to note where the dark material ended and the white-tan sand began. Stabilizing himself on one leg, he poked his free foot over the edge.

The sand barely gave any resistance at first. He had his shoe buried up to the toe before he had to apply pressure to dig deeper.

A blaring, discordant noise behind him made him jump forward, trying to spin on the soft surface. He flailed his arms to keep his balance, ending in a fighting crouch. The car that had made the awful noise kept speeding down the roadway.

Ari needed to be more careful. He would get plenty of practice walking on sand as he made his way toward the town. He checked his watch once more before setting out.

# Chapter Two

The bamboo wind chimes above the door to The Old Oak clattered as a new customer stepped in. It *had* to be someone new, because all Sarah's regulars knew this was her cleaning weekend.

The restaurant and yoga deck below were closed while she scoured the treehouse from top to bottom—and did her yearly arbor upkeep, which she planned to work on that afternoon. She headed out from the kitchen, wiping her hands dry on the back of her shorts.

"Hi. We're actually..." Her voice trailed off as she saw the man standing near the door.

Standing wasn't the right word. Looming? Towering?

He filled the entire entryway to her treehouse restaurant. He was bald, without a hint of stubble on his chin and jaw that she could see. His skin was dark amber and his shoulders as broad as the door. His head was dangerously close to the ceiling fan.

Her treehouse was small, but the ceilings weren't *that* low.

He was holding his wrist, his back mostly to her, and

glancing around as if he was confused. That plus the bright red shirt covered in pictures of toucans and palm trees, and she was pretty sure he was a tourist.

The small art district where her tree grew wasn't really on the beaten path, and few tourists stopped by—especially in the off-season. He must be lost. She moved forward to see if he needed help, but froze again when he turned around and fixed her with his dark gaze.

He was absolutely gorgeous.

"Hi." He dropped his arms to his sides and cast a brilliant smile at her.

She felt the strangest urge to curl her toes.

"Um, hi." Wait, hadn't she already said that? She shook herself inwardly. "We're actually closed today. There's a diner around the block, though. They have pretty good coffee."

"Coffee? Oh, no." He grimaced and shook his head. "No coffee for me."

"You don't like coffee?"

"I tried it once. It had a profound effect on my physiology." He shook himself as if trying to get rid of a bad memory, then smiled again.

Was he making a joke? She couldn't quite tell. There was something odd about him. Something intriguing— beyond his build. And his build was…amazing.

She would *love* to have a profound effect on his physiology.

She had a brief flashback to her days in the corporate world. Back then, she'd been so busy building her career that "relationships" were mostly a string of one-night stands when she felt like a little company. It had been a long time since she'd felt like company.

"I prefer kale smoothies," she said. "I get the same energy boost without the jitters."

"That sounds much more pleasant."

"I'd make one for you, but—"

She paused as she noticed the duffle bag slung over his shoulder. It couldn't hold much, so he was traveling light. Sending him away didn't feel right. Plus she'd only had the lizards who lived in her tree to talk to that day. They weren't the best conversationalists.

Maybe a little company was just the thing.

"You know what?" she said. "Have a seat. I'll make you one."

"I don't want to inconvenience you."

"This is a restaurant. Why else would you be here, if not for the food?"

She laughed, but he didn't join in for a few beats. It was just long enough to make her wonder about him even more. But then he dropped his bag on the floor and sat on a stool next to the bar that ran between them.

She wrote it off as him being from out of town.

"I'll be right back," she said.

He interlaced his fingers and leaned on the counter. "I'll

be right here."

In the kitchen, Sarah began humming to herself, trying to puzzle out the mystery of the newcomer. Cerulean was basking on the windowsill, gazing at her with his gold eyes. Violet was on the counter, glaring. Sarah hadn't known lizards could give people the stink-eye until she'd met Violet.

"Violet, get off of there."

Sarah reached for the emerald lizard, but wasn't fast enough to grab her. Violet scampered up the wall, making her way to one of the kitchen shelves that was out of Sarah's reach. All that was up there were old cookbooks Sarah rarely used.

"If you're going to keep sneaking into my kitchen, at least hang out on those empty shelves above you so you don't make a mess," she said. "And stop running around on the counters. You're going to get me in trouble with the health department."

Sarah knew it was ridiculous to address the lizards as if they understood her, but they were *always* around now, and she'd gotten into the habit of talking to them. She grabbed a cloth and wiped down the surface, then headed to the sink to wash her hands.

The lizards were remarkably tidy. Violet was the only one who liked to make messes. Usually she would knock over containers. With how big the reptiles were, Sarah was glad they all seemed to be housebroken, but that didn't mean they were clean. She was trying to train them to stay away from the food surfaces.

She didn't mind that they had basically taken over her tree and the loft where she lived above her restaurant. Sarah liked having other living beings around to talk to. Still, it would give her some peace of mind if she could figure out exactly what they were.

They looked like a cross between an iguana and a green basilisk, but they all had bright silver stripes running down their backs and along their arms, tails, and sides. The silver stripes were so uniform, they almost seemed artificial, like someone had painted them on.

They had other stripes as well—more natural-looking, with uneven patterns. Sarah had named her new friends based on the color of those stripes. Cerulean was the nicest and would even ride on Sarah's shoulders sometimes when they were up in her loft.

Violet, though. Violet had it in for Sarah.

She had never heard of a lizard with a strong personality, which was part of why she wanted to know what they were. But any time she tried to get a picture of one, it would vanish. Her lizard friends were remarkably camera shy.

Cerulean let out a hiss from his spot on the windowsill. Sarah turned just in time to see Violet knock a cookbook off the shelf.

"Dammit, Violet!" Sarah leapt out of the way as the heavy book bounced off the counter and narrowly missed crushing her toes.

"Is everything okay in here?"

Sarah spun around to find the stranger standing in the kitchen doorway.

"Yeah, just...problems with the wildlife." She gestured toward the shelf where Violet had just been lurking, only to see it empty. Sure enough, the windowsill was vacant as well.

She let out a deep sigh. "There really were two lizards here a moment ago."

"I believe you." He gave her another thousand megawatt smile, laugh-lines framing his lips.

Very nice lips...

"I've seen dozens of small reptiles running around outside," he said. "They're everywhere. It's incredible."

Definitely a tourist.

"I'm not talking about the little anoles. These guys are big. Huge. I have no idea what they are. They just showed up one day and made The Old Oak their home. I mean, not the restaurant. Though they do tend to hang out here. But they live in the tree, and...I'm rambling."

She never rambled. Unless she'd had a couple of drinks, which she hadn't done in years, actually. This guy was hitting her system like a double shot of whiskey.

He smiled at her in response. Probably didn't want to set off the crazy lizard lady. That's what one of the yoga instructors had jokingly called Sarah when she mentioned the lizards that no one else ever seemed to see.

She should raise the rent on the deck space below when they wanted to use it for classes. But that would be petty.

Sarah picked up the cookbook and stared at the high shelf. Normally, she would climb up and kneel on the counter to reach it. She wanted to avoid doing that in front of a handsome stranger, even if it would put them at more of an even eye level. And lip level.

She shook off the thought and said, "I don't suppose you'd put this back up there for me, would you?"

"Sure."

Her request turned out to be a mistake. At least, if she wanted to minimize the effect he was having on her. He stepped forward and took the book from her hand, filling the kitchen with his presence.

The room was small. That made preparing food easy when she was working in it alone. She barely had to take a step to reach every surface, every storage space she needed. With him inside, it seemed *miniscule*. There was no place to go to give him room.

His shirt brushed against her, surrounding her with the scent of him. Soap and...evergreen. Not part of the soap. He smelled like the pine needles and snow in the mountains where her parents lived.

She tried to step out of his way as he put the book on the shelf, but ended up tripping over his foot. He caught her, his hands warm on her bare arms.

"You okay?" he said.

She might be, except that she couldn't stop thinking about how soft and strong his hands felt. Her belly flooded with warmth, tingles building between her legs with a speed that shocked her. He was setting her off in ways she had missed more than she realized.

She should really get out more.

"I'm fine," she said. She even managed a smile and an awkward laugh.

"I'm glad to hear it."

He was dusting his thumbs across her skin. She didn't think he was aware of it, the way he was staring down at her.

Maybe he was thinking about kissing her. She really, really wanted him to be thinking about kissing her. But then he laughed and shifted away, back toward the door to the restaurant.

*Damn.*

"Actually, I should probably go," he said. "I just arrived in town and need to find a place to stay."

She tried not to let herself be disappointed. This guy was an Adonis. He was covered in muscles. His clothes were brand new and very high end, even as casually dressed as he was.

Sarah's hair was held up in a quick ponytail. Her tank top and shorts undoubtedly showed off both her overly abundant curves and almost total lack of muscular definition.

She couldn't tone up anywhere no matter how hard she tried. And she had tried. She'd had dreams of competing in the Olympics when she was a kid. Before several ill-timed growth spurts, her gymnastics teachers had thought she had a chance.

In the two decades since then—had it really been that long?—she'd worked out sporadically, but only really started taking care of herself after selling her startup company and retiring at a ridiculously early age. She'd made peace with her body, her focus shifting to feeling healthy rather than trying to meet society's standards. If she wasn't this guy's type, she wouldn't hold it against him.

It was a shame, though.

"There's a hotel right across the street," she said. "It's a little Bohemian, but the owners are really nice. Or there's another place closer to the main part of town. You'd probably want to call a cab to go there. It's a bit of a hike."

He smiled at her and her train of thought came to a screeching halt. Somehow, she knew that smile would always stop her dead in her tracks.

"The place across the street sounds great."

"Let them know I sent you." It probably wouldn't make a difference. She was still rambling.

"I'll do that." He turned and headed out the door.

She took a few deep breaths. Her body was tingling all over and she had the strongest urge to run after him, grab him, and kiss him, just to see what would happen.

She didn't even know his name.

"I *really* need to get out more," she said.

When she turned around, she saw Cerulean sitting on the windowsill again.

"There you are. Where were you a minute ago, when I looked like a crazy person talking about giant lizards?"

Cerulean cocked his head to the side in a quintessentially reptilian fashion, then blinked. The blue stripes along his sides deepened and he straightened his front legs, letting her know he wanted a ride.

"Fine, but only while I'm cleaning inside. When I'm trimming the tree, you need to give me space to stay safe."

She let out a frustrated sigh as she walked to the window and held out her arm. He climbed up quickly and perched across her shoulders.

"I can't stay mad at you." She ran a finger gently over his cheek. "Violet, though… She's on my shitlist."

Sarah swore Cerulean's lips pulled up in a smile.

"I *am* a crazy lizard lady." She shook her head and got back to work.

# Chapter Three

This mission was going to be more complicated than Ari had thought. The readings seemed to be centralized around a tree. An *inhabited* tree. He had never heard of such a thing. Earthlings certainly were innovative with their living spaces.

There were thousands of different species in the Coalition of Planets, but he didn't know of any who lived in trees. Not even the Tau Ceti, whose planet was a swamp covered in enormous vegetation.

He'd wanted to ask so many questions, but was afraid she might grow suspicious of his ignorance. The hotel owners had been forthcoming enough to satisfy most of his curiosity.

According to them, living in a tree wasn't all that common on Earth, either. The Earthling—Sarah—lived and worked in the house that had been built into the enormous plant. She operated a restaurant on the lower level and lived above in what was called a loft.

Ari liked the small spaces in her home. They reminded him of the spaceships where he'd spent most of his life.

The natural materials of the building added a warmth that he particularly enjoyed.

The large deck that surrounded the base of the tree was used by people in the community who taught classes on health and something they called "spiritual wellness". Apparently, Sarah had designed the entire thing and had it built when she moved to the area.

Her accomplishments beforehand also impressed the hotel owners, but Ari didn't quite understand what they were talking about. Something about owning a materials company and holding her own in a global marketplace. He'd kept smiling and nodding, which seemed to mask his ignorance.

The owners of the hotel had spoken of Sarah warmly while showing Ari to where he would be staying. They had apologized for the size of the room, not realizing he was used to having only a bunk with a regen bed to sleep in and a tiny storage locker for his backup uniform.

All he had asked for was a room that overlooked the "treehouse". The rest of the details were insignificant. He needed to get more readings. He needed to study the dwelling. Ari had been amazed when he first saw it, staring more at the building than the data his watch was feeding to him.

The deck underneath the restaurant was decorated with colorful fabrics and small candles and sculptures arranged in a manner that was oddly pleasant to look at. He had felt an unfamiliar sense of peace from simply observing the setting.

A few tables with built-in benches were scattered about the open ground surrounding the tree. They reminded him of the tables in the *Arbiter's* mess deck.

A spiral staircase led up to the restaurant. He wasn't sure how the loft above was accessed. He needed to get closer. He needed to study the structure. But that meant he needed to interact with the Earthling more.

That was a problem.

Maybe it was the odd emotional effects of viewing the treehouse, or the shifting ground beneath his feet, but Ari *felt* something when he was with Sarah. Something strong enough to divert his focus unacceptably.

The *Arbiter* had been full of rumors about General Serath—Adam—and his bondmate. Soldiers said they would come across the pair kissing in corners of the ship.

Ari hadn't believed any of the stories. Why wouldn't they wait to reach the General's private quarters to kiss? The need for discretion would surely be stronger than their bodily urges.

Then he had come across them himself—huddled in a corner, forms tangled as they seemed to be trying to press themselves as close to each other as possible. Ari had retreated quickly, wondering what could drive them to do such a thing.

At the Department of Homeworld Security headquarters,

Vay and Henry were always holding hands or touching when in any kind of proximity—even though it was impractical to hold hands while walking. And Ari had come across Zemanni and Brooke in more compromising positions than he wanted to remember. None of it had made sense.

But after meeting Sarah…

Ari could imagine kissing her in the corridors of the *Arbiter*. Or in the closeness of her kitchen.

He'd never encountered anything like the softness of her arms. Sparring with his fellow Sadirian soldiers, his opponents felt solid, muscles taut right beneath their skin. Their flesh didn't yield like Sarah's had—almost as if it were inviting his touch.

"What *is* it about this place?" he said.

He wanted to touch more of her.

Her skin was gold from the sun, like the highlights in her brown hair. Her eyes were dark, like his. And her smile…

He shook his head. He shouldn't be thinking about her smile or her skin or how hearing her gentle voice made him want to do nothing more than listen to everything she said. He had a mission.

Activating the scanners in his watch, he headed outdoors again.

The heat was a welcome change from the chill of Brendan's mountain estate. His room at Homeworld headquarters was uncomfortably spacious compared to where he'd be staying during this mission. Ari was even getting used to the shifting sands, especially after walking around the tree to pinpoint his readings.

He glanced across the street and halted.

Sarah was up in the tree. High up. She was climbing along the branches, holding some sort of tool. Her movements were graceful as she weaved among the branches, but she still should be using a safety harness.

If she'd been over the treehouse or the soft sands, he wouldn't have been as concerned. But she was out at the edges of the tree, with nothing but the deck thirty feet below.

This was not his world. She had to know what she was doing.

But physics worked the same everywhere.

He forced his attention back to his watch, scanning for more of the strange readings, trying to ignore the unsettled feeling in his stomach. Moments later, he heard Sarah scream.

He ran toward her without thinking, his heart pounding as he watched her fall through the branches. They slowed her descent, but not enough. He was too far away to catch her, and with her velocity and the hardness of the deck...

Five feet before impact, her body slowed. By the time she landed on the deck, most of her inertia was gone. She hovered above the wood for a moment, then lowered onto it, like someone was gently setting her down.

An antigravity field. No wonder she'd felt safe working in the tree without a harness. But where had she obtained it?

His stomach twisted. What if *Sarah* was the invading alien he was looking for?

Many species would modify their appearance over generations after entering the Coalition until they looked almost indistinguishable from Sadirians. The Tau Ceti were a prime example.

They had modified themselves to the point that they could walk among Sadirians—and Earthlings—without being noticed. Which made it easier for them to prey on humans.

Since humans were from a lost colony ship that had crashed on the planet millennia ago, humans didn't need to change their appearance to look Sadirian. Technically, Sadirians and Earthlings were the same species—if Sarah *was* an Earthling.

He shook himself. If she wasn't, then he would arrest her. It was as simple as that.

When he reached her, he realized it was complicated.

Her eyes were wild, her chest heaving. Tears streamed down her face. As he knelt at her side, he could see her entire body was shaking.

"I'm alive. How am I alive?" she gasped. "I don't understand."

"Stay calm."

He tapped his watch quickly, activating the scanners to check her for injuries. Slowly passing his hand over her body, he found that she was unharmed, aside from a few mild lacerations from the branches hitting her back, legs, and arms as she fell.

Closing her eyes, she took a deep breath, then let it out slowly.

"Nothing hurts," she said. "And I can feel my legs."

"That's good. You have some scrapes and bruises, but otherwise you're okay. Let me help you up."

"I'm a big fan of Reiki, but I think I'm supposed to lie still until the paramedics arrive."

Bringing in other authorities might scare off whatever aliens Ari was hunting. He needed to avoid that if possible, and he knew that she was uninjured.

"What is ray-key?" He asked the question to buy time, but was gratified when she laughed.

"You're definitely not a local. Reiki is a healing technique. It's a form of 'laying on hands'."

"Humans can heal each other through touch?"

"'Humans'?"

Moons, a slip like that could jeopardize his mission.

"Oh, that was weird," he said. "Seeing you fall has shaken me. I can only imagine how you feel."

"I feel…fine, honestly. A little awkward, though. I want to sit up, but if the adrenaline is covering injuries that aren't hurting yet, that could be very bad."

"You aren't in danger due to your fall." Other sources... He wasn't sure yet. He locked her gaze with his, then picked up her hand and squeezed it. "I promise to keep you safe."

He wasn't sure where that had come from, but he meant it.

"How crazy is it that I believe you?" She laughed briefly, then she pulled on his hand, starting to sit.

He wrapped his free arm around her as he stood, bringing them both to their feet. She burrowed against his chest, wrapping her arms around him. That was... unexpected.

Warmth spread through him. He held her close, offering comfort as she calmed herself. He'd seen Kira and Brendan stand like this, and had thought it strange. Experiencing it himself, he understood their affection much better.

After a moment, Sarah pulled back and looked up at the tree. "Seriously, how am I okay?"

She truly didn't seem to have any idea what had happened. But then, how *was* she okay?

"The branches must have slowed my fall enough to protect me," she said. "I was looking for dead limbs that needed to be trimmed. Thank God I had only just started, or I would have fallen on a pile of pointy sticks."

She still wouldn't have been injured. Someone had used technology not available on this planet to stop her fall. But who? And why?

The Coalition provided soldiers with handheld antigravity units that could be used both to move small heavy objects and to immobilize prisoners, depending on the setting of the device. They could easily be concealed in someone's hand. But no one was in the vicinity.

Whoever it was had protected Sarah. Very likely saved her life. There was more going on here than he understood.

"Let me help you inside," he said.

"I'm okay. I think I'm going to go upstairs and lie down for a while."

He wasn't sure which bothered him more—not being able to study her environment and conduct more thorough scans, or not being allowed to help her.

"But—"

She reached up and touched his cheek, silencing him. He felt her trace his lip with her thumb, the touch feather-light, but hitting his senses like a shock cannon. His skin tingled as if an electric current was passing close. Blood rushed to his groin.

He leaned closer.

She was still breathing quickly, adrenaline no doubt flooding her system, obscuring her judgment. He didn't have an excuse for his own reaction to her.

"I don't know your name," she said.

"Ari."

"Ari."

His name on her lips came out as a sigh, like the wind in the new leaves of the tree above them. He wanted to hear it again. Closer—whispered in his ear.

"Let me make you dinner," she said. "Tonight. After I've had a chance to settle down."

"Sure."

*Wait, what did I just agree to?*

It was hard to focus with her smiling up at him. He wasn't used to feeling such a pull toward anyone. He'd been attracted to other shipmates—had even been involved with a few. None of them had affected him like Sarah.

This situation was even more complicated than he'd thought. Looking into her eyes, he doubted it would become less so as his mission progressed.

# Chapter Four

After several hours of lying in her bed, watching Cerulean…watch *her* as she stared at him, Sarah had come to a decision. She was going to seize every day and live it for all she was worth.

She had nearly died.

Near death experiences often inspired people to make changes. She'd thought she had already found her path to happiness. Now, she wasn't sure.

Moving here, she'd been looking for more than a home. She wanted to be part of a community. The people were great, but somehow, she didn't feel connected to them. She helped them and they visited her restaurant or used the space below, but she still felt like an outsider.

Corporate life hadn't been enough for her. She'd been there, done that. Running her own company had been great, but she hadn't felt like she was making enough of a difference there, either. She'd hoped that helping people individually, face-to-face, might give her more satisfaction. Building The Old Oak was part of her plan to save the world, one person at a time.

She came up with sustainable recipes that were easy on the environment and extremely nourishing for her customers. She taught classes about vegetarian cooking, and had even branched out into vegan recipes.

The Old Oak was a center for the community. Sarah vetted each class, interviewed every teacher, to make sure their teachings were supportive of a better world.

Sure, it was *Sarah's* vision of a better world, but her tree —her rules. And insisting that people be respectful to themselves, each other, and the environment didn't seem like such an extreme position to take. She wanted to help people find balance and happiness. Including herself.

And in honor of that cause, she had spent the remainder of her day in the kitchen, singing to herself—well, and her lizard friends—and cooking her favorite dishes to share with Ari. She wasn't convinced that he wasn't interested in her anymore. Tonight, she'd find out.

"Sarah?"

"Coming." She quickly grabbed the last dish from the counter, then headed for the restaurant.

Just like the first time she'd seen him, Ari took up most of the Old Oak's entryway. He was even in the same outfit. Apparently, if he thought of this as a date, he wasn't the kind to dress up for it. She sort of liked that.

She, however, had cleaned up. After a brief but soothing self-spa session, she'd put on her favorite dress. It was made from a deep green fabric with a faint leaf pattern. The dress had a flowing skirt and halter-top with spaghetti straps. She hadn't bothered with a bra, but had picked out her favorite lace panties. Just in case.

She'd left her hair down and her feet were bare. The simplicity of it made her feel comfortable. And she could be naked in seconds, depending on how the evening progressed. She wanted to be able to seize the moment if it came up.

Ari's eyes widened when he looked at her. It made her feel like the most beautiful woman on the planet.

"Uh, hi." He grasped his wrist, covering his watch as he dropped his arms in front of him. It seemed to be a habitual gesture.

"Hi." She smiled, pushing away the nervous thoughts at the edges of her mind. It had been a long time since... Actually, she'd never done something quite like this. "I have us set up around the corner."

"Okay."

Most of her customers would take their food outside and eat on the picnic tables around the treehouse. Some sat at the counter and chatted. There was also a small round table in the treehouse that could seat four.

And then there was *the nook.*

Ari followed her to the small table that was nestled into the little alcove in the treehouse. It only sat two. Customers could call ahead if they had a special dinner planned and she would decorate it for the occasion. She'd never decked it out for herself.

A string of clear lights illuminated the space like tiny stars, and a gauze curtain hung from the ceiling to give a better sense of privacy, even though it was only the two of them with the restaurant closed. The curtains were pulled apart so that she could easily come and go, since she was the server, chef, and diner that evening.

Most of the food was already on the table. She added the last dish and gestured for Ari to sit across from her. He didn't try to pull out her chair, which was a relief. She always felt awkward when guys did that on dates.

Ari sat and looked around at the lights, then to the food resting on mismatched, colorful plates. His knee jutted out from his chair and he barely seemed to fit in the nook space. She could reach across the table and touch him without even stretching. Then again, that was sort of the idea of the spot.

"Are you feeling better?" he asked.

"Yeah. I'm just a little banged up and stiff. It's still kind of a miracle. I keep thinking maybe I wasn't as high as I thought or something."

"You were at the top of the tree." His brow was furrowed and his expression grim. "I watched you fall, but was too far away to do anything."

"That's probably for the best. If I'd landed on you, I would have squished you." She was trying to lighten the mood, but he kept staring at her with that dark expression.

"I would have caught you."

"Then I would have fallen into a trope."

"Trope?"

She shook her head and laughed. "Forget it."

"Why weren't you using a safety harness?"

"I've never needed one before. I know how to operate in a tree. The only reason I fell is because of Violet."

"Violet?"

"She's one of my lizard friends. Frenemy, more like. I'm pretty sure she's trying to kill me."

Ari sat straighter in his chair and glanced around the room, as if looking for threats. Maybe he was a soldier. His gestures and movements reminded her of people she'd known who had served in the military. But still, she was talking about a lizard.

"Ari, I was joking." Sarah laughed. "Violet is a lizard. Lizards don't try to kill people. Unless they're a Komodo dragon or something, and planning on eating us. And I seriously doubt Violet wants to eat me. I hope not, anyway."

"What do these lizards look like?"

She shrugged. "Have you ever seen an iguana?"

"No."

"How about a green basilisk? They're the funny-looking lizards that can run across small stretches of water."

The crease between his eyebrows deepened.

"Okay, that makes it harder to describe. My friends are

bright green and have different colored stripes down their sides, sort of like a tiger." She paused and smirked at him. "Unless you've never seen one of those, either."

He paused for a few beats before he smiled. It was just as dazzling, but seemed forced.

There was no way he had never seen a tiger. Iguanas and basilisks, she could understand, especially if he was from up North. But a tiger? Who had never seen a tiger?

Shaking away the uneasy feeling that gave her, she went on. "Anyway, their heads are rounder than most lizards, with more of a...forehead, I guess. And they have these little crests on the backs of their skulls, and a short spiney fin that runs down their backs. I think they kind of have a fringe around their faces as well."

"Hold on a second." He started tapping on his watch. It had a black band and a large, flat face. Definitely high-tech and high-end. After a few moments, he cocked his head to the side, his smile vanishing. "How tall are they?"

"Tall? Don't you mean 'long'?"

He smiled again, but somehow it seemed like a diversionary tactic.

"Yes, of course."

*Of course.*

Sarah was a pretty good judge of character. She hadn't sensed anything from Ari that made her think 'crazy person'. Not yet, anyway. He was starting to push it, though.

"They're about six feet long. Half of that is their tails." She looked over to the closest window, sunlight fading through the branches. "I wish I could show you one. They're really beautiful. But no one else has ever seen them. I can't even get them to hold still to get a picture. They seem to just *vanish*. Do you think you know what they are?"

"Hmm?" He was staring at the floor, his right arm resting on the table.

Sarah glanced at his watch and saw a weird screen with a picture of a green basilisk lizard on it. The picture wasn't the weird part, even though it looked kind of like a hologram. The bizarre symbols made up of loops and wedge-shapes scrolling on the side—that was weird.

Ari caught her glance and covered his watch briefly. When he moved his hand away, the surface was blank.

She'd studied many cultures while learning about holistic health practices. The closest form of writing to what she'd seen on his watch was cuneiform, but she was pretty sure people had stopped using that a couple thousand years ago. *Human* people.

Stifling a laugh, she shook her head.

Everyone misspoke sometimes. Ari's earlier lapse— referring to "humans" as if he wasn't one of them—after she'd fallen from the tree had been weird and a little endearing. She was relieved to know he wasn't as perfect as he looked. But it had given her imagination too much to work with.

For a moment, she wondered if the symbols on his watch were some sort of alien language. Maybe he was a bounty hunter looking for her lizard friends. Well, her lizard friends and *Violet*.

Or maybe the lizards were the aliens. Sarah could imagine a story where Violet was a criminal mastermind, out to take over...the treehouse?

Violet did seem to have a mean streak. If she hadn't jumped out of the leaves—appearing from nowhere—Sarah wouldn't have fallen at all. It had almost seemed like Violet had startled Sarah on purpose.

A chill ran down her spine.

She was being ridiculous. Lizards did not have vendettas against people—against anything. And the markings on Ari's watch... They were probably some kind of computer code.

Most importantly, she was *not* surrounded by aliens.

She forced herself to smile, remembering what the evening was supposed to be about. "We should eat before the food gets cold."

Ari cast a strained smile back.

# Chapter Five

The meal in front of him smelled amazing, but was completely bewildering. Ari wasn't sure how to eat anything. None of it looked like the rich foods that Brendan served at Homeworld headquarters. Ari didn't know where to start.

He wished he could tell her the truth, but that was impossible. Perhaps he could give her just enough of the truth to help him with his current predicament.

"I'm not from here," he said.

"I guessed that," she smirked at him. "You're from a place that doesn't have tigers or iguanas and people communicate with a different alphabet. If you had an accent, I'd think you were from another country."

"I currently live in a home in the Absaroka Range in Montana. And the symbols on my watch..." He searched for more that he could share. "My watch was developed by one of the most brilliant communication technology experts on the planet."

She nodded, as if that didn't surprise her in the least. "So, you're with the military."

"Yes." It was true. He was a soldier for the Coalition.

"Well, you can't weaponize my lizards."

"Excuse me?"

"You were curious about them." She shrugged, then smiled.

He smiled back, his face relaxing a bit.

"Ah. They just seem interesting."

More than interesting. They sounded like Vegans. But Vegans were only legends. They supposedly hadn't been seen in the Coalition for thousands of years. Not since just after the High Council was formed.

Vegans had helped to found the Coalition after their own homeworld had been destroyed. To survive, they had poured all of their efforts into science and technology. Their race had still been devastated, and the few remaining Vegans had headed deep into space in what they'd called the Life Ship.

According to legend, Sadr-4 had become their home for a time, but after seeing that the High Council no longer needed them, the Vegans had headed back into space to find other races to recruit for the Coalition. Instead, they had vanished.

Ari had learned quite a bit about the Coalition since he'd first heard stories about the Vegans. Somehow, he doubted that the legend told the whole story—if *any* of it was true.

The Life Ship was said to be a paradise, with a self-sustaining ecosystem that supported the Vegans' reptilian physiology. They supposedly liked dense foliage and high temperatures.

Ari looked out the window at the green leaves that nearly blocked the warm rays of the setting sun, even this early in the spring.

"You won't see one," she said. "They're very good at hiding."

Sarah's voice pulled him back to the room—away from his ridiculous train of thought. The Vegans weren't real. They were a story meant to bolster morale and instill obedience in other species. "Only the High Council had access to Vegan technology, making them the chosen ones of the Vegans." It was just propaganda.

Then again, the Tau Ceti had recently been found to have technology that far surpassed that of the Coalition. No one had figured out where it had come from yet, but it was doubtful they developed it themselves.

Zemanni had also had technology that was beyond anything their team had ever seen, but said that he'd bought it from what Henry called "the space black market". Zemanni didn't know where it had originated—just that it had given him an edge in his bounty hunting.

Ari shook himself inwardly. The Vegans were a legend. And even if they weren't, they most certainly wouldn't side with the Sadirians' enemies. It was too terrible a concept to think about. A traditional "scary story" told while sitting in front of a fireplace, like the ones Brendan had introduced them to.

Sarah was real, and sitting right across from Ari. She'd welcomed him into her beautiful home, helped him find shelter, and made him this feast. He needed—wanted—to keep his focus on her.

"I'm sorry," he said.

"It's okay. The food might seem intimidating, but I promise you, it's all good."

He laughed and looked back to the food. "I've never seen anything like this. I don't know where to begin."

"I can help you there."

She scooted her chair closer, sitting more next to him than across the table. Their legs were almost touching. It made it hard to concentrate on what she was saying.

"These are the appetizers."

She pointed at what looked like a tiny brown orb made up of plant matter and filled with diced vegetables and... something else. Then she gestured to a pool of tan puree next to several triangles of what he recognized as a form of bread.

"What are those?" He pointed at the tiny brown bowl-food-thing.

"Quinoa-stuffed mushrooms with vegetables and parmesan. And these..." She picked up one of the bread triangles and a spoon, then scooped some of the puree onto it and placed it on his plate. "These are a treehouse specialty. Homemade hummus and pita—somewhat fresh from the oven. Trust me, it's delicious."

He didn't doubt it. And it would probably leave him feeling weighed down and half-sick, the way the rich food at headquarters always did. Ari sometimes missed the simplicity of the nutrient bricks they ate aboard the *Arbiter*.

She prepared a few more of the triangles, then turned to him and smiled. Whatever expression she saw on his face made her burst into laughter.

"Oh wow, you look so nervous." She gestured back to the plates and said, "It's just healthy food. I promise it won't hurt you."

"Right."

Maybe her healthy cuisine wouldn't have the same effect as the cooking of Brendan's chef. Ari picked up his fork, and Sarah laughed again.

"The fork is for the main course. You can eat these with your fingers. Here." She picked up the mushroom, then brought it to his lips.

Did she mean to feed him? The idea was bizarre. If it was a custom, though, he didn't want to risk offending her. He opened his mouth and let her pop in the tiny bite of food.

Her expression was so hopeful, he steeled himself against the taste to make sure he could at least look like he was enjoying it. Rolling the thing on his tongue, he discovered he didn't need to pretend.

He bit into it and felt like his mouth was filled with earth and light, heightened by the freshness of the vegetables and sweetness of…something else. He wasn't even sure what he was eating. The sharp salty tang of the cheese tied the flavors together.

"Do you like it?" she said. "Please tell me you like it. You look so focused…"

"What?" He swallowed reluctantly after mumbling around his food. "It's amazing. I've never had anything like it." He wished there was more.

"Here, have mine."

She picked hers up and started toward him again, but he caught her wrist. Heat streaked through his body at the touch, her skin so soft against his. He stared at her intently, plucking the mushroom from her fingers.

Following the apparent custom, he leaned forward till the morsel brushed against her lips. Her eyes widened, but then she opened her mouth and let him feed it to her. The skin of her neck had turned pink, the color spreading across her cheeks as she chewed.

This didn't seem like simply sharing a meal. He remembered how it had felt when she brushed her thumb across his lips earlier. What had that meant?

The other Sadirians on Earth had warned him that the cultural indoctrination program was insufficient. He knew several slang expressions, and their communication was improving. But there were so many customs and idioms to learn.

Feeding each other like this felt…intimate. There had to be some sort of significance to it.

The arrangement of the table in the odd shaped room gave them each a small space in front of them for their plates while the majority of dishes sat out of the way to the side. Their chairs had started facing each other, though at a slight angle, and close enough that they could lean forward and kiss.

His stomach dipped at the thought, a thrill flooding through him not unlike entering a planet's orbit in a high-G maneuver. She had moved her chair closer. Close enough that he could feel the heat from her skin.

She picked up one of the triangles of bread and leaned forward. Their legs brushed, but instead of moving away, she let her knee rest against his thigh. Her skirt didn't reach that far. Their bare skin pressed together.

He shifted toward her without thinking, keeping the contact, letting her knee push the fabric of his shorts higher. His dick was stiffening and he didn't know what to do about it.

Well, he had *some* ideas.

Gossip on the *Arbiter* covered this, too. Earth sex. How humans would join their bodies naturally, without needing chemical assistance, like *Coupling*—the drug the Coalition provided to citizens to satisfy their needs.

Ari had never joined in with the chatter—never wanted people to know that he had tried sex with a few partners without using the drug. They had all consented to his odd preference, but had wanted to use *Coupling* themselves.

The experiences had been unsatisfying.

It wasn't about the climaxes. Those were fine. The issue he had was with knowing that he didn't even need to be there for his partner, and they didn't need to be there for him. It seemed so pointless.

But just the thought of sliding into Sarah, of feeling her muscles clench around him, knowing that her responses would only be because of *him* and what he was doing to her, what they were sharing with each other... *That* would have purpose.

His neck tingled. His skin felt alive with that strange sensation of unguarded electricity hovering close. It spread across his shoulders, up to his cheeks and down his chest.

Could this be what had caused her cheeks to redden? He glanced at her shoulders and chest to see that her skin had a flush to it that covered everything he could see. And he could see more than he'd realized at first.

Her dress was dark green, with thin straps holding it up at the shoulders. Her chest was exposed, the tops of her full breasts gleaming in the pale light.

What he could see was softness. Fullness. Another texture that he wanted to experience, with his hands, his mouth...

She ran the bread across his lip. He let her feed him another bite.

# Chapter Six

Sarah watched Ari's eyes drift shut as she fed him another piece of soft pita bread. She knew food could be a romantic and sensual experience, but this was so far beyond that.

After getting past the self-consciousness of someone watching her eat with such a high level of intensity, she started feeling the act as a sort of connection. It was like sex, but through feeding each other.

How had she never tried this before?

The bread was still warm. She'd made sure to time baking it so they could enjoy it when it was fresh.

Ari slid another bite into her mouth. She must have eaten this a thousand times, but she'd never noticed the creamy texture of the hummus in quite the same way. If he didn't make a move soon, she was going to jump on him.

His hands lingered near her face, fingers trailing down her cheeks and along the sides of her neck. He hesitated briefly before shifting his touch to her arms. For a moment, she'd been sure he was going to cup her breasts.

She picked up another piece of pita, wishing she'd made

more and wanting to move on to what she hoped came next at the same time. Their gazes locked as she fed him, tracing her fingertips over his lips, then over the strong muscles that flexed as he chewed.

He dropped his hands to her legs, warm fingers sliding along her thighs before gripping them tighter and pulling her onto his lap so that she straddled him.

*Okay, that was just the right amount of pita.*

She rested her forearms on his shoulders, leaning close, imagining how his lips would feel on hers—how he would taste.

"Sarah."

She wanted to keep watching his lips form her name. She wanted to kiss them. To feel them on her body. But she pulled her attention back to his eyes.

He slid his hands further up her thighs, under her skirt. Squeezed the softness of her hips and pulled her closer, but not quite close enough.

"This seems like an invitation," he said. "But I don't want to misread the situation."

She ran her fingertips along his temple, across a strong cheekbone, then over his lips. "If you think this means I want to have sex with you, you're not misreading the situation at all."

"Thank the stars." He finally pulled her tight against his dick, taking her lips with his in one graceful movement.

Absolute bliss.

He pressed himself against her, wrapping one arm around her lower back to hold her close and gripping the nape of her neck. His hand was so big, he could easily encourage her to tilt her head to the exact angle he wanted. He kept his touch gentle.

She needed more. More skin on skin, more heat.

Reaching between them, she quickly unbuttoned his shirt and pulled it open. He hissed in a breath when she pressed her hands against his chest, following the curves and valleys of his muscles with her fingertips.

She kissed along his neck and he leaned back in his chair, eyes closed. She took the opportunity to explore him with her gaze, her fingers, her lips. The loose fabric of his shirt had hidden how perfectly he was formed. She'd never been with someone so *built* before.

She shook herself internally, pushing away her self-doubt, telling herself not to question this experience. She wanted to revel in it.

Whether it was to be a fleeting encounter or the start of something deeper, she reminded herself to be in the moment, to feel everything. She wanted them to enjoy each other fully.

But not in her restaurant.

She rose to her feet, though she could feel her legs trembling. The intensity of his gaze made the fluttering in her stomach erupt into a wave of heat that shot through her body.

"There's a ladder in the kitchen that goes up to my loft," she said.

He nodded, then stood up as well, towering over her. She led him to the ladder that was set into the wall.

Ari climbed behind her gracefully, skipping every other rung. As she opened the trap door in the ceiling, she wondered what he would think of the tiny loft where she lived. He would only be able to stand all the way up in the exact center of the room, if that.

Her desk was built into the wall in front of the biggest window. Her bed took up most of the remaining space. Her few personal belongings—mostly books and clothes—were under the bed in plastic tubs to keep the moisture and bugs away. Not that she'd seen any bugs since the lizards had moved into her tree.

A tiny bathroom was just past the even tinier closet, fed through a rainwater reservoir on the roof. She had just checked the tank that morning, making sure the water looked clear and nothing was leaking.

The pale green throw on her bed complemented her sage sheets. She had put up more of the strings of tiny clear lights all over the space, lighting it with a soft glow.

Ari pulled himself up through the trapdoor and sat on the floor, looking around with a smile on his face. He rose in a crouch and took a few steps to the window, looking out at the tree, then turned back to the room, still smiling.

"It isn't much, but it's home," she said.

"It's wonderful."

He rolled onto her bed and stretched out with his arms behind his head. Closing his eyes, he let out a deep sigh. He seemed completely relaxed in the cramped environment. It was odd how easily he moved in the confined space.

His shirt had fallen open, driving that line of thought from her mind. She enjoyed the view for a moment, then sat next to him on the bed. His steady breath and broad smile helped calm her nerves.

It had been a long time since she'd had sex. Even longer since she'd made a move on someone she'd known for such a brief time. This still felt like the right choice, though.

Taking a soothing breath, she sank into the sensations her body was feeding her, just like in her yoga practice, deeply connecting her awareness with her body. She reached for his chest again, trailing her fingertips over his muscles.

"I'm surprised at how comfortable you are in the treehouse," she said. "Were you assigned to submarines or something?"

His eyes opened, a crease appearing between his eyebrows.

"Or something." He picked up her hand and pressed it against his chest. "I can't—"

"Talk about it." She nodded. "Yeah, I get it. I just... I guess I'm trying to learn a little more about you. I don't usually invite guys I've just met into my bedroom."

He sat up, bringing their bodies close. Her concerns scattered.

"Why did you, then?"

She searched for the right words before answering.

"Have you ever met someone and they seemed familiar right away? As if you could feel your future with them rippling back through time and letting you know that something was there? Something important?" She realized how that sounded, and immediately backpedaled. "I mean, not a long future or forever or anything. Just… You know, like this. Us being here."

She was rambling again.

He nodded, and said, "I've felt that before."

"Oh."

Her stomach sank.

"This morning. When I met you."

"Oh…"

He opened his mouth, but closed it again without speaking. He let out a deep sigh before he spoke. "I don't want to mislead you. I feel something strong between us. But I'm not going to be in town long. I can't stay."

Her chest constricted. She was surprised she could be so disappointed when they had only just met. All the hope that she didn't even realize was building around him toppled onto her, making it hard to breathe.

Some people would have lied just to make sure they wouldn't scare off a potential lover. Ari was giving her a chance to cut her losses and walk away. But she knew she wouldn't.

If their time was that limited, she didn't want to waste any of it.

# Chapter Seven

This was insane. Ari was considering disobeying orders and telling Sarah everything. About his mission, the threat to Earth, that he had been born—created—on a space station orbiting Sadr-4. All of this after a few conversations and a shared meal.

After a kiss.

Kira had warned him that Earth could be bewildering. He'd had no idea how accurate that was.

"I don't think—"

"Good." Sarah grabbed his shirt and dragged it over his shoulders and down his back. "We need to stop thinking. Both of us."

*Stars, that sounds wonderful.*

He shrugged his shoulders free of his shirt, leaving it behind in her hands. She tossed it aside, then wrapped her arms around his neck, her lips seeking his out for a searing kiss. His hands flexed on the back of her dress as her tongue slid into his mouth.

Dinner had been a glimpse of what this could be. He understood that so much better now.

He did his best to match her movements, stroking her tongue with his, sucking it. She let out a groan, pressing herself against his chest.

Gripping the straps of her dress, he pulled them down her shoulders. She straightened her arms, helping him to peel the garment from the top of her torso. Her nipples had firmed, contrasting the softness surrounding them. He had to see. To touch.

Her areolas were large, a slightly darker shade than her olive skin. He cradled her breasts reverently, using his lips to caress her nipples. He drew one into his mouth, stroking it with his tongue.

Her fingers dug into his shoulders and she gasped. Her hips rocked against him, as if she was as desperate as he was to feel his dick buried in her.

He rolled her onto her back, then sat at the edge of the bed so he could pull her dress over her hips and down her legs and cast it away. She was wearing an intricately woven undergarment of rich brown that hugged her hips and gave him a tantalizing glimpse at her skin beneath. So little was between them.

He unfastened his cargo shorts, then kicked off the loafers, sending a silent "thank you" to Brendan at the ease of their removal. He paused as he remembered their last conversation, and the "special supplies" Brendan had given him. Condoms.

"Just in case," Brendan had said. "Earthlings seem to

have quite an effect on Sadirians."

Ari had never dreamed he would use them, but was grateful again. They were in the oversized pocket on the right leg of his shorts. He stood, hunched over in the small space, and pulled out the box, then set it on the bed.

"I'm glad you're prepared, because even if I had condoms that were less than a year old, they would not fit you."

Sarah was staring at the hard ridge of Ari's dick pressing against his shorts. She scooted to the edge of the bed, and sat in front of him. The intensity of her gaze sent more electric thrills through him.

"May I?"

He wasn't sure what she was asking for, so he said, "Sure," hoping he could figure it out along the way.

She gripped the sides of his shorts and pulled them down far enough for gravity to take over. After he stepped out of them, she flung them aside. Then she pressed her hand against his shaft.

His chest constricted. He had to fight to steady his breath. Feeling her hand through the thin fabric of his undergarment, knowing her entire focus was on him, her body and senses primed for him… It was almost too much. He took several slow breaths to calm himself down.

She traced his dick with her fingers, helping it to turn upright before pulling the waistband of his boxer-briefs down slightly. As soon as his crown was exposed to the balmy air, she ran her fingertips lightly over his heated skin, sending shooting waves of pleasure across his nerves.

He reached for her to…pull her away? Closer? He wasn't even sure. But when he reached her hair, the softness of it added to the sensations cascading through him. He buried his fingers in the featherlight strands, gently stroking the sides of her neck.

She leaned forward, maybe as off balance as he felt. At least she was sitting. He didn't want her to fall again.

Instead of leaning against him, she brought her tongue to his dick, stroking it in a quick motion before sucking the tip into her mouth.

"Stars…" he breathed.

She pulled down his boxer-briefs, letting his dick fall from her mouth, but running her cheek along its length. The softness of her skin against such a sensitive part of his body sent pulses of pleasure through him, thrumming along his nerves. He managed to step out of his undergarments, staring down at her in awe.

This was what it was like to share each other's bodies. Sensation, pleasure, touch. He'd never experienced such intimacy.

She brought her hands around to cup his ass, squeezing his muscles, then nuzzled his dick again. "I've never heard someone use 'stars' that way, but I like it."

He couldn't even bring himself to fault his lapse. Nothing could diminish this moment.

"I want to see if I can make you say it again." She smiled up at him as she ran her tongue along the underside of his dick.

He groaned, tightening his grip on her hair, being careful not to pull it. He just needed to feel grounded, to experience what she was doing to him with as much of his body as possible. She circled his crown with her tongue, then sucked his dick deep into her mouth.

"Stars," he grunted out. "Oh, stars, Sarah."

She intensified the pressure of her tongue, swirling it along his shaft. She pushed on his ass, encouraging him to move against her.

Carefully, he thrust his hips toward her, then pulled back. Every micrometer of movement shuddered through his body. He had never known such bliss.

Earthlings were innovative. So innovative. He would never have thought to touch someone like this. Even though he hadn't always used *Coupling* with his partners, he had never touched or been touched this way.

He kept thrusting against her, his dick sliding in and out of her mouth as her tongue lapped and swirled. She moved her hands to his ribs and lightly scratched her fingernails down his abdomen.

More new sensation.

He let go of her hair and pressed his arms against the ceiling to stabilize himself. She grasped his shaft with one hand, squeezing it tight as she kept sucking on his tip.

Pressure was building in his groin, a nexus of pleasure in his dick and balls nearing critical mass. If they didn't stop, he would go off, and then this beautiful experience would be over. He wouldn't be able to share more with her, feel himself inside of her.

He started to pull back, but she tightened her grip, circling her fingertips around his sac. It was too much. The last bit of sensation sent him over the edge.

He exploded into her mouth, pleasure arcing through his body, pounding along his nerves in time with his heartbeat. He thrust against her mouth as she quickened the strokes of her tongue, drinking him in, pumping her hand along his dick.

"Sarah!" He could barely keep his balance, was only able to breathe her name.

The lights seemed to dim, the floor shifting beneath his feet. He slid from her mouth, and dropped to his knees in front of her, panting.

Wrapping his arms around her waist, he rested in her lap, trying to pull himself back together. Her touch was light on his shoulders. She traced the muscles of his back, ran her fingertips along his spine.

"I'm sorry," he finally managed.

Her hands stopped. "For what?"

"For not lasting longer. For finishing so quickly." He couldn't bring himself to look at her as he sat back on his heels. He kept his gaze on the floor.

Sarah laughed. "I'm amazed you lasted that long. I was using all my best moves on you."

He looked at her then, saw the brightness in her eyes.

The experience they had shared was so far from how things were done among his people. On every level.

Partners would take a dose of *Coupling*, then writhe next to or against each other, sometimes not even joining their bodies, and the drug would automatically take them through the stages of arousal and climax. He'd always had to rush to even enter his partner before they would finish, and usually ended up bringing himself to fruition on his own afterwards—an act he kept absolutely secret.

What he'd considered a brief sense of unity with his shipmates was nothing compared to what he'd shared with Sarah.

Was this enough for her, though? He had wanted to lay on top of her, to feel their bodies pressed together and joined in the most intimate way.

"I don't understand," he said.

She leaned forward, running her fingers along his cheekbone.

"That," she said, "was the appetizer."

# Chapter Eight

The look on Ari's face as he thought through Sarah's statement was almost its own form of foreplay. His eyes widened, his mouth dropped open, and then—after a moment—he smiled at her.

Not one of his beaming megawatt smiles. It was a devilish smile. One that made her wonder what he had planned.

His earlier reaction had been strange, though. It was almost as if he'd thought the night was already over. If she had anything to do with it, they'd still be enjoying each other the next day.

His body wasn't even the most amazing thing about him. The way he used it, the way he seemed to want to feel everything, experience being with her so fully… It was a little intoxicating.

He leaned forward and kissed her again, one hand burrowing through her hair to hold her close, the other going to the small of her back and pulling her toward the edge of the bed. His tongue delved into her mouth, thrusting as vigorously as his dick had a moment ago.

He moved his mouth to her neck and shoulder, then across her chest. He lifted her breasts and massaged them, sucking her nipples, stroking them until the ache between her legs became an intense throb. She'd never had someone get her off just through working her breasts. If anyone could, it would be Ari.

He let out a sound that was half-growl and pressed a kiss to her stomach, then hooked his fingers over the sides of her panties and pulled them down her legs. She fell back onto her elbows. He stared at her core for a few moments, his chest heaving with each breath.

How the hell was she working him up so much? And she'd thought that she wasn't his type. She'd been wrong. Really, really wrong.

He fixed his gaze on hers as he lowered his mouth to the curls between her legs. He pressed a kiss to her, keeping their gazes locked. Then he trailed the backs of his fingers along her slit.

She knew she would be wet, but was surprised when he slid one of his large fingers deep into her, her body accepting him easily. After not having sex for so long, she thought she'd need more of a warm up.

*Slow down, Sarah.*

She *did* need a warm up. He was huge, and—wet or not —she wasn't ready for him.

He sat back, dropping his gaze to her core as he used his thumb to part the folds of her flesh. "Stars, you are beautiful."

A frisson of pleasure snaked through her body that had nothing to do with his hands on her. Okay, it had a little to do with his hands on her. But it was more that she kept getting him to use that odd expression—that being with her was making him lower his shields.

*Because, you know, he's an alien.*

She laughed inwardly at her earlier thoughts about his watch. Her imagination had really been running wild.

She turned her attention back to him—what he was doing to her. Anticipation built along with the pleasure he was stoking with his hands. He leaned forward and added his lips to the mix.

She fell back on the bed. As she stared at the tiny white lights above, she let herself sink into the sensation of him. He thrust his finger deeper, kissing her clit, then circled it with his tongue.

Electric arcs of sensation darted out from where they touched, lighting up parts of her that she'd ignored for too long. She brought her feet up to rest on the edge of the bed and trailed her fingertips over his scalp to encourage him.

"I need more before I'll be ready for you," she said.

He slowed his movements briefly, his breath hot against her clit. "More?"

"I want you to be able to slide into me," she said. "I'm still too tight."

She gasped involuntarily as he withdrew his finger and

moved his hand to her hip. He rose up onto the edge of the bed, hooking her thigh over his leg as he easily shifted her entire body back to give himself more room. His dick was already beginning to harden again.

He brought his thumb to her clit, circling it as he watched her face intently, then he slid his finger back into her. Slowly, he added another.

Her breath caught in her chest, her back arcing off the bed. He started to pull away.

"Don't stop," she said.

He paused briefly, then thrust his fingers deep.

She let out a sigh. "Oh, stars…"

She managed to catch his gaze long enough to smile at him. He smiled back and his hesitation vanished.

He leaned down to kiss her neck as his hand continued to thrust between her legs, pumping faster, his thumb swirling around her clit. The arcs of electric pleasure were shooting through her nerves faster, more frequently. He bent his head to her chest, somehow balancing on his elbow to not crush her as he lifted her breast against his mouth, sucking her nipple in deep.

That was enough. The energy he'd been building exploded in a white-hot burst of fireworks along her nerves.

Her back arced further, her hips bucking against his hand as he kept thrusting his fingers into her, grinding against her clit with the heel of his hand. She writhed on him, pulling every ounce of pleasure she could from his touch, from his kiss. Heart pounding, body singing, she finally collapsed back on the bed.

He pushed her closer to the middle of the mattress and pressed his chest to hers, his dick rock-hard and prodding her thigh.

"Condoms," she said.

He looked confused for a moment, as if he was so caught up in the moment that he'd forgotten them. But then he grabbed the box and tore it open, fumbling with the foil packets inside. She picked one up and opened it, rising so that she could help him put it on.

*Stars, he's huge.*

She smiled at her own thought, loving both the expression and that using it felt so natural to her.

It didn't matter if being with him was a short-term thing. She knew she wouldn't be the same after this. Being with him—in and out of bed—had changed her.

When his dick was covered, she gripped his shoulders and lay back, pulling him with her. He held himself up on his elbows, their chests touching, though he kept his weight from crushing her.

His eyes squeezed shut as he slid into her, slowly parting her flesh. He stretched her so far, her body ached from it in the best possible way.

She was already throbbing around him, ready to go off if he moved even a little. He held himself there for a moment, giving them both a chance to adjust.

"That feels too good," she said.

"Agreed." He pressed himself deeper, his hips grinding against her clit. "I'd like to experiment."

Her stomach flipped nervously. "Experiment how?"

"Different movements. Positions. I want to learn what gives us each the greatest pleasure."

"Sounds like a noble cause."

He sat back on his heels, keeping her tight against his dick by holding onto her hips and drawing her up his thighs. She wrapped her legs around his waist, feeling him slide deeper into her. With the pressure off of her clit, her body backed away from the edge a bit, giving her more space to enjoy the feel of him.

Drawing his dick out slowly as she angled her hips away, he moaned, then slid back in. He seemed to be savoring this experience as well. He put his hands under her thighs to help hold her up, pumping faster.

Her core stretched to fit him, tugging on his dick every time he pulled out, her belly filling with pleasure as he thrust himself back in. Heat uncurled through her, building along with the pressure between her legs.

"I'm not going to last much longer," he said.

She wasn't either. She slid her hand between her legs, swirling her fingers over her clit. His eyes widened, watching her add to the pleasure he was giving her, slamming into her faster and harder. A final deep stroke sent her over the edge, her back flexing, driving her shoulders down into the mattress as she called his name.

He let out a grunt, then started pounding into her. Her core hugged his dick, pulsing around it, coaxing even more out of him. The waves of her climax went on and on.

Finally, he fell forward, catching himself on his elbows to keep from crushing her. His dick was buried so deep, stretching her, filling her. Echoing pulses sounded faintly along her nerves as their bodies calmed. She couldn't tell which were from her and which from him.

"That was the most amazing union I've ever experienced." He nuzzled her ear, then pressed a gentle kiss against her neck. "Thank you."

"Anytime. Like, seriously." She let out a deep sigh and shook her head, feeling herself relax deeply. "That was…"

Ari glanced over at the pile of foil packets next to them. He looked back at her and grinned. "An appetizer."

# Chapter Nine

Earth wasn't bewildering. It was fantastic.

Ari stretched, feeling Sarah shift next to him and curl closer to his side. The sun had risen hours ago, but they hadn't left the bed. Except for the interlude when she stood, leaning forward against it. And then against the wall when he'd intercepted her coming back from the bathroom.

They had only managed to keep their hands off each other long enough to run back downstairs and eat, and take brief naps between sessions of unity. Sometimes, they stayed awake afterwards and talked.

She had led a textile company—one that focused on sustainability and quality. After conquering that challenge, she had turned her attention to helping people in this community. Teaching them to live in harmony with themselves, each other, and the world. Her values were directly in line with what he and the Department of Homeworld Security were trying to accomplish.

He was learning so much. He would never get enough of this—of her.

She was beautiful and smart. Funny and so giving. She

knew what she wanted and wasn't afraid to go after it. For all of her gentleness, he sensed strength like the hull of a starship within her.

He wanted to learn more, especially about what they could become. But he would have to leave eventually. He would have to leave *soon*.

"I want breakfast," she said. "But I also don't want to get up. It's a dilemma."

He laughed, stroking her hair away from her face. "Food is important. Come on."

He helped her up, then swung his legs over the side of the bed. How long had it been since he'd checked in with Kira? He needed to take care of that right away.

"Why don't you go downstairs and get started," he said. "I'm going to run to the bathroom and then I'll join you."

"Okay." She leaned forward and kissed him, lingering a bit. Then she sighed and crawled across the bed. She picked up her dress from the night before and pulled it over her head, then shimmied into her panties.

"Do you really think those are necessary?" He loved the idea of being able to slide into her whenever they wanted, without any more delay than putting on another condom. Which they were running low on, now that he thought about it.

"I don't want to be tempted. No sex downstairs." She smirked at him, then said, "But breakfast won't take long."

"Sounds good."

He waited for her to disappear down the ladder to the kitchen before grabbing his own clothes and heading for the bathroom. After using the facilities and quickly dressing, he activated a secure communications channel to Kira, keeping his watch close to his lips and speaking as quietly as he could.

"Your report is two hours late." The voice was male. Not Kira. "What have you found?"

"Rin? Where's Kira?"

"Dealing with the newest shitstorm."

Of all the Sadirians on Earth, Rin had most readily adapted to human curse words. Embraced them, even.

"Emergency meeting of the First Contact committee," Rin said. "I mean Department of Homeworld Security."

Ari could almost hear Rin rolling his eyes—a gesture he'd picked up from Brendan's sister, Paige.

An emergency meeting could mean many things. None of them good.

"Have we located the Centaurans finally?"

"That's the least of our problems. We received a coded transmission from Adam. Apparently, the High Council is reviewing his report on the Tau Ceti threat, but think it's been blown out of proportion. He hasn't even broached the topic of the changes to our society that we're hoping for or recognizing Earth's Department of Homeworld Security."

Ari's stomach sank. This was beyond bad news. It was potentially catastrophic, for Earth *and* the Coalition.

The High Council had backed themselves into a corner without realizing it. They controlled every aspect of Sadirian life—even designing the DNA of the citizens they approved for creation.

Drugs like *Coupling* and *Balance* were meant to keep everyone in line, but they also dulled creativity and prevented innovation. Nothing new had been developed within their culture for thousands of years. They were still coasting on the technological developments that had hurled their people into space—and let them dominate every sentient species they encountered.

Most sentients only joined the Coalition for access to the technology—or if the High Council used their technology to force them to. But some of those sentients had taken it upon themselves to make improvements. Like the Tau Ceti. They were a threat, and one the High Council shouldn't disregard.

"What's Adam going to do about it?" Ari said.

"That's not our problem. The High Council is concerned about his interest in Earth. They're sending a replacement ship to investigate whether the planet needs to be brought into the Coalition early."

Cygnus X. That would destroy the Earth and subjugate humanity in a way most Earthlings couldn't imagine.

"What ship?" Ari said.

"The *Reckoning*."

The last bit of hope Ari had held onto faded. He put his

hands on either side of the sink and bowed his head.

When there was a chance for a peaceful resolution, the High Council sent in the *Arbiter*. It was meant to be both a show of strength and mercy. If Adam could resolve the situation through diplomacy, he would. And the ship was fully armed in case a stronger course of action was needed.

The *Reckoning* was sent in when the Council wasn't bothering with diplomacy. Commander Teisha was known for her swift decisions and brutal enforcement of Coalition law. She did as the High Council said, and if they wanted Earth brought into the Coalition, it would happen.

"Ari, are you there?"

"Yes. What are my orders?"

"I don't know. This is happening kind of suddenly. The *Reckoning* was on assignment in a distant system, so we have a few weeks."

It didn't seem like enough time to accomplish anything. Except enjoy his last few hours with Sarah. He doubted he would see her again after this.

"I'm going to continue my mission," Ari said. "I haven't figured out the source of those readings yet."

"Well, hurry up. Kira might call you back here the moment their meeting is over."

"Understood."

Ari terminated the transmission.

Moons. What could he do to help Earth? To protect it— and Sarah—from this?

He had traveled with the *Arbiter* to hundreds of Coalition planets. They'd all been stripped bare, trading their natural resources for access to the technology the High Council promised.

And when their planets couldn't support life anymore, and all the people were huddled under domes, the High Council stepped in to help, managing the population, genetically engineering people who could survive on less and perform specific duties—for them. The Council was only saving sentient species from situations that they had helped to create.

There had to be a better way.

"Hey, Ari?"

Sarah called to him from the trap door that led below. He cleared his throat, before calling back.

"Yeah."

"Could you come down here?"

"Sure."

He had a mission. He needed to focus. But he also needed...Sarah.

It had been twenty-four hours since they'd met, and he already couldn't imagine spending a day without her. Now that he knew what his colleagues were experiencing, he understood their choices so much better.

He climbed down the ladder into the kitchen. Sarah was standing near the sink.

"Did you come down here and clean up last night?" she

said.

"No." He wouldn't even have known how. Brendan had people who took care of all the cooking and cleaning in the mansion where they were all living.

Sarah opened the door of the refrigeration unit and peered inside. "All the leftovers are in here. And the counters are cleaned, the dishes done and put away." She turned back to Ari, her brow furrowed.

He shook his head and lifted his hands briefly. "It wasn't me."

"This is so weird. Maybe I did it in my sleep last night." She closed the door and shook her head. "But that would mean I'm closer to actually being a crazy lizard lady than I'm comfortable with."

He wrapped his arms around her shoulders, drawing her closer. "You're not crazy."

"Thanks, but I'm starting to wonder. I mean, who would come in here just to clean up and put my food away? And why am I the only one who ever sees the lizards in my tree?"

"I'll help you figure it out."

He had a feeling when they did, his own questions would be answered. Like, who had used an antigravity field to save her life the day before and why?

Her head was resting on his chest and she was facing the window. A wave of tension flowed through her body. They had become so attuned, it was impossible to miss.

"What is it?" he said.

"Shh. Don't move."

He didn't know what threat they faced, but followed her order.

"It's Cerulean," she said. "Don't scare him off."

Ari's heart thudded in his chest. Cerulean was one of the lizards she had told him about—the ones that sounded like Vegans. But that was impossible. Vegans weren't real. He turned his head as slowly as he could, trying to not scare whatever it was away.

Sunlight fell through the leaves, casting a scattered pattern of light and dark on the creature's bright green scales. It crawled from the windowsill onto the counter, staring at them.

She hadn't exaggerated its size. It would be just about three feet tall standing on its hind legs.

As it dropped to the floor, another lizard came through the window. And another.

"Please tell me that you see them too," Sarah said.

"I see them." He could barely believe it himself.

Each had stripes along their sides in vibrant colors. Cerulean's were a rich blue like the sky outside. The second one to come through the window had somewhat greener-blue stripes.

And then there was Violet. He recognized her immediately from Sarah's stories. How could a lizard look...angry?

Their stripes didn't catch his attention as much as the strip of silver running down their backs, along their limbs and tails, and framing their rib cages in a design that was too even to be natural.

Exo-suits. Just like in the legends.

"Solar Cross..." he whispered.

He let go of Sarah and slowly lowered himself to one knee, placing his right hand flat on the ground and bowing his head in a show of supreme respect.

"I know I told you not to scare them off," Sarah said, "but this is a little—"

She let out a little choked sound as the first Vegan, Cerulean, rose onto his back legs. Ari dared to lift his gaze enough to watch.

The silver stripes along Cerulean's back and limbs popped off of his body, becoming three-dimensional as they remolded themselves to his frame. He opened frills along his jaw and neck, which pushed his eyes forward so that his face looked flatter and more humanoid. His tail lifted behind him, flicking back and forth as he stretched into a bipedal posture.

"Stars..." Sarah whispered.

The other two Vegans stood as well, transforming in a similar fashion, until they were standing before them, looking like three tiny green people. With tails. And scaled skin.

"Greetings, Sadirian," Cerulean said. "We are pleased

that you honor us in the presence of our chosen Protector."

Ari had to swallow a few times before he could speak. "Protector?"

"Yes." Cerulean smiled, his green lips stretching across his face. "The Earthling Sarah."

*Oh shit.*

# Chapter Ten

"So, I've gone insane." Sarah let out a high, brief laugh.

"This isn't what you think," Ari said.

He was still kneeling in front of the lizard people.

*Lizard people.*

"There are three little green men standing in my kitchen."

Cyan cleared her throat. "Actually, Violet and I are female. We thought we had conveyed this."

Sarah laughed again. She remembered Cyan making little irritated clicks at Sarah the first few times she'd used the wrong pronoun. They had been communicating without her even realizing it.

Violet let out a string of clicks and hisses that sounded distinctly unhappy.

Sarah was trying to maintain some sense of being grounded. She focused on her feet and the cool wood of the floor. On Ari's reassuring presence close by.

"Enough." Cerulean cut Violet off with a brusque wave of his hand. His tiny green hand.

"Speak so that Sarah can understand you," Cyan said.

Violet narrowed her eyes, her lips curling back from the rows of sharp teeth filling her mouth. She'd never been shy about communicating her dislike of Sarah.

"What is your deal?" Sarah said. "Why do you hate me?"

"You are not worthy." Violet bit out each word.

"Harsh." Sarah shook her head, which was a bad idea. The room was already kind of spinny. "Wait, worthy of what?"

In a much gentler tone, Cyan said, "Of being our leader."

"What?" Ari's voice joined with Sarah's as they spoke at once.

Ari sprang to his feet, shaking his head. "Sarah is an Earthling."

"We are now of both Vega and Earth, as is Sarah," Cyan said. "She is the bridge between our two sentient species."

Ari shook his head. "There's been a mistake."

"There is no mistake," Cerulean said. "She made the offer. We have accepted. Earth shall become our new home."

"What offer?" Ari and Sarah again spoke at the same time.

"You welcomed us with your placard," Cerulean said. "And then confirmed the invitation through your digital communications."

"Wait, wait, wait." Sarah put her fingers to her temples,

pinching her eyes shut for a moment. "Are you talking about email?"

She thought over the emails she had sent and received in the past few months. A few from friends, most from family, and some business emails...between her and the mysterious tech company that had out-of-the-blue started helping her because they were fans of her restaurant.

"Are you my new *web designers?*" Her voice rose to a ridiculous level by the end of her question.

Cerulean stood straighter, the blue stripes along his sides becoming more vibrant. "Our efforts have improved your operations on many levels."

Ari finally turned his full attention back to her. "Did you hire them to build some sort of web device for you?"

"No," she said. "I mean... They made me a new web site."

He stared at her blankly.

"You know, on the Internet?" she said.

"Of course." He did that thing where he smiled just a moment too late. "The Internet."

She might have bought it if he hadn't added that last part. But he was trying too hard.

He didn't know what a web site was. When they'd first met, he'd been confused about what The Old Oak was— he'd seemed confused when she offered to make him food after entering a restaurant.

The markings on his watch, little things in their

conversations from the night before. And most telling of all, how Cerulean had called him "Sadirian".

"You aren't human," she said. "You're an alien. You're all aliens."

"I can explain." Ari was holding his hands out toward her as if to fend off an attack. He didn't bother trying to deny it.

"We are aliens," Cerulean said. "We were clear. And you expressed your desire to join us."

Ari's eyes grew wider. "You did what?"

She started to laugh. She couldn't help it. Nothing felt real, and the situation was utterly ridiculous.

She remembered the email correspondence she'd had—apparently with Cerulean. It had been a back-and-forth conversation that had been going on for a few weeks now. Sometimes he'd been *sitting on her shoulder* during their exchanges. He must have had a way to reply instantly, reading her messages over her shoulder.

He *had* seemed pretty squirmy sometimes.

She laughed harder as she imagined him with a teeny phone, typing in messages behind her back so she couldn't see. The laughter kept building, becoming impossible to control. Her sides hurt, tears streamed down her face.

"I said…" She gasped for breath, trying to force out the words. "I said I wanted to be a vegan."

Ari turned to Cerulean, and said, "A vee-gan? What is that?"

"An Earthling who does not consume the flesh or by-products of other animals." Cyan sniffed. "It is spelled in a similar manner to Vegan."

"Similar?" Violet hissed. "The word is identical."

"It was capitalized on the placard outside her dwelling *and* in her digital communications," Cerulean said. "We have the records. In English, proper nouns are capitalized, therefore, she was referring to a native or citizen of the Vega system, rather than the more general earth term."

Sarah was holding her sides. The room was spinning. She might be hyperventilating.

All of this was because of a sign she'd put out to advertise a change in her menu and a type-error in an email she'd written hastily.

"Vegans Welcome," she said, wiping at her eyes as fresh tears rolled down her cheeks. She mispronounced the word on purpose, just to hear out loud what they had interpreted. "Vay-guns."

"She obviously meant these…vee-gans," Ari said. "This will not stand with the Coalition."

"Do not lecture me on Coalition law, Sadirian." The frills around Cerulean's face started to quiver.

Sarah couldn't believe that the tiny lizard was able to intimidate Ari, but the huge *Sadirian* bowed his head.

*Oh my God. I had sex with an alien.*

"I mean no disrespect," Ari said. "I speak only as a warning. I'm here because we detected odd readings around this tree and the surrounding area. Earth has been invaded by many trespassing sentients who mean to harm both Earthlings and their ecosystems."

"Wait…" Sarah shook her head. "What now?"

"There's a group of us working for Earth's Department of Homeworld Security," he said.

"Home*world*?"

He nodded.

Her laughter had vanished. A heavy dread filled her stomach instead.

"I think I need to sit down," she said.

Ari picked her up and set her on the counter, keeping his hands on either side of her legs. She could feel him staring at her, but didn't want to meet his gaze. Not yet.

She took a few deep breaths, then said, "When you came into the restaurant yesterday, looking at your watch, you were investigating those weird readings."

"Yes."

There was that honesty again. She had thought he was being straightforward with her. Now she knew he was hiding so much.

"Is that why you stayed last night? To get a closer look at the place?"

"What? No. Not at all. Sarah…" He gently lifted her chin.

His eyes were such a warm brown. Lines of concern were etched at their edges, and the smile she found so disarming was gone. He was frowning deeply instead.

"I stayed because I wanted to be with you. To be closer to *you*. It wasn't about my mission or any of this."

"You didn't tell me you were an alien."

"I couldn't. And would you even have believed me?"

She might have. She'd had suspicions.

The important thing was that she believed him now. She pushed away the tangled knot of emotions twisting through her stomach, and focused on what she understood about the situation. What she knew about him.

He had run to her aid when she'd fallen. He'd been overjoyed to talk about ways to improve the quality of life for the people in her community, advising her to increase her efforts to help more people. That made more sense now.

Everything did.

He wanted to help Earth, to help *humanity*. Little snippets of their conversation came to mind, where he'd spoken vaguely about where he was from. He'd let her know that he wanted to help others as well. His people. Other...aliens.

She was in this deep. Little green men—and women—were standing in her kitchen, looking to her to see what would happen next. They were probably wondering if her mind would snap at the sudden weight of all this knowledge. Maybe they thought she'd be too afraid to do anything but what they told her to. Violet would probably love that.

But that wasn't Sarah.

She slid off the counter and turned to face Cerulean. She took Ari's hand in hers. Standing next to him helped bolster her confidence.

"Why are you here?" she said.

Cerulean folded his hands in front of his green body. "You invited us."

"That's not what I meant. Why were you on Earth in the first place?"

"We were not on Earth." Cyan stepped forward. "We were in the vicinity, conducting scans of your planet. We, too, noticed many sentient species, and thought perhaps Earth had begun inviting beings from other planets to live here. The ecosystems are diverse and the planet is rich in resources. It could easily support a variety of lifeforms."

Violet let out a string of hisses and clicks. Cerulean wheeled around and responded in kind. Their tails lashed back and forth behind them, and they crouched as if they might attack each other.

"Peace." Ari held up his free hand. Both reptiles turned to him, their eyes narrow, pupils barely visible slits. Ari tightened his grip on her hand and shifted closer to her.

Hadn't she seen this in some movie? It hadn't ended well for the human…ish people. Even tiny lizards—in large groups—could take down large prey. There were at least a dozen Vegans living in her tree.

And of course they were carnivorous, based on how the

bugs had vanished after they moved in.

"Let's focus here," Sarah said. "You were poking around and saw my sign and decided to move in. Is that about right?"

"Yes." Cerulean cast a withering stare at Violet, who merely hissed at him in response. "We have observed your planet, your peoples, and their diverse civilizations. Earthlings are on the cusp of a great shift. One that we wish to nurture and support. And we have been wandering for too long. We wish to rebuild our society, integrating with the Earthlings when their own development can handle it."

"Solar Cross…" Ari said.

Sarah was missing something. Something big, based on how Ari was acting. "There are only a dozen of you. How do you expect to rebuild your society?"

"There are a dozen serving the Protector and living with you in your tree," Cerulean said. "The rest are on the Life Ship."

Ari gasped. "The Life Ship is here? On Earth?"

"It is cloaked, off of the coastline."

Sarah shook her head. "How many people are we talking about?"

Accidentally inviting a dozen lizard-aliens to live with her in her treehouse was one thing. Letting Earth be overrun by an alien species was another.

"Two hundred and fifty thousand." Cyan looked at the ground, her shoulders hunched. "Our entire population."

"That's all?" Sarah's heart lurched in her chest.

It didn't matter that they were vastly different life forms. She could feel Cyan's grief—all of their grief—filling the tiny room.

There were *cities* in Florida with more people than that. And that was just one state in one country on one continent.

"Our numbers have dwindled over the generations," Cerulean said. "If we can not make Earth our home, we face extinction unless we take...drastic measures."

She didn't like the sound of that. Neither did Ari, based on the way he stiffened beside her.

Violet, on the other hand... Violet might be smiling.

"We have been looking for a new home for a very long time." The hope in Cyan's voice, and the way she wrung her tiny hands in front of her chest, were heartbreaking.

"I don't have the authority to invite you to live here," Sarah said. "I mean, surely you've spoken with our leaders or something."

"You are a leader in your community, and that is where we will begin. When we have finalized our arrangement, we will approach your First Contact committee."

Her mind was reeling. She wanted to help Cerulean and his people. But she had no idea what she was getting herself—or her planet—into.

She shook her head. "I don't know what to say."

Ari took in a quick breath, his grip tightening on her hand. He leaned down so he could whisper in her ear. "Say 'yes'."

# Chapter Eleven

Ari had a plan. The beginnings of one, anyway. A plan that would protect Earth *and* the Vegans. Moons, if things worked out as he hoped, he and Sarah could help all of the sentients in the galaxy. *All of them.*

But only if she could trust him.

"How can I do that when I have no idea what I'd be saying 'yes' to?" Sarah said.

"I know more about the situation than I can tell you right now." He turned to her, resting his hands on the warm skin of her arms. "But you know *me*."

"Do I?"

He winced under her glare, but then nodded. "I understand that this situation must be overwhelming. Believe it or not, I feel it, too. But there's much at stake here. More than you can imagine."

"Oh, I can imagine a whole heck of a lot." She looked over at Cerulean and his group, a tiny furrow between her eyebrows.

She was focused on protecting Earth and helping the Vegans. He was sure she would do what she could to that end. But she didn't know that the *Reckoning* was on its way.

Earth was about to become the center of alien politics, one way or another. If the Vegans wanted to offer Earth their protection, it might give the Coalition pause. It could buy them time to figure out some other solution than letting the entire human populace know about aliens and all the promises—and hidden dangers—they presented.

"You trusted me when you fell from the tree yesterday," Ari said. "Please trust me now."

Her lips tightened and she frowned, but then she nodded.

He turned to Cerulean and said, "May we have a moment?"

Ari couldn't believe he was addressing a Vegan—that they were *real* and right in front of him. He stood tall, waiting for their response.

The one who seemed to be their leader—Cerulean—bowed his head slightly. "We understand your need to speak with your mate in private."

"Mate?" Sarah said. "Oh, no. He's not my mate."

Cerulean cocked his head to the side. Violet hissed out a laugh.

"Then he has no business being part of this," she said. "Sadirian, it is *you* who are trespassing."

Cerulean held up his hand to silence her. "The Sadirian has also been welcomed by the Protector. Only she can determine his role. We will be waiting outside."

The three of them walked to the window, then scampered up the wall and over the sill. They disappeared into the foliage of the oak.

Sarah sagged against Ari as soon as they were alone.

"What the hell is going on, Ari? Is that even your name?"

"It is. I have a designation number as well, but Ari is easier to remember."

"A designation number. Great."

She leaned into his chest and he dared to wrap his arms around her shoulders. He hadn't been sure she would ever let him do so again, and let out a small breath of relief.

"Listen to me, Sarah. There is more going on here than you realize."

She snorted. "You keep saying that. Let me just sum up what I *do* realize. There are all kinds of aliens on Earth, several in my tree, one in my bed. A group of Earthlings is working with your people—Sadirians—while the Vegans want to work with me specifically."

"That's only what's going on at the surface."

"All of this has been dropped on me before breakfast. I kind of figured there are more factoids for me to discover."

He hugged her closer, another level of tension dropping away when she hugged him back. "I want to help you. I want to protect you. I promised I would keep you safe."

"You didn't know what was going on then. About the

Vegans or the Life Ship. About any of it."

"I still meant what I said. But this isn't just about you or me or us anymore. Earth's future is at stake."

"So, no pressure or anything." She sighed and stepped back, looking up at him. "Who am I to make this decision? And honestly, who are *you* to help me make it? Some bounty hunter here to track down a few rogue aliens?"

"I'm not a bounty hunter." He spoke more harshly than he'd intended, but didn't like the reference, what with a Scorpiian living at the mansion with them now. Ari managed to take a bit of the edge off his voice when he spoke again. "I am a soldier in the Coalition's fleet. I have served for my entire life. I was created for this purpose. Keep that in mind when you hear what I'm about to say."

He gripped her arms lightly, made sure she was looking him in the eye. "I am concerned about the trespassing species on your planet. I am concerned about the danger you pose to yourselves as you learn to balance your technological needs with preserving the resources of your planet. But the greatest threat is the *Coalition*. It is the greatest threat that Earth has ever faced."

"The Coalition? But you work for them."

"Which is why I know what I'm talking about. They will tempt your people to ruin. Fan the flames of greed and avarice. And when you've traded all the resources of your planet for the technology they offer, the only thing you'll have left to give is yourselves."

"My God... That's awful."

"One of the most advanced ships in the fleet is on its way. When it arrives, the commander will not bother with stealth. She will not bother with diplomacy. She will decide that Earth has been irrevocably contaminated and contact whichever government leaders she thinks will facilitate Earth being brought into the Coalition. Those individuals will get to decide the fate of the entire planet."

"But she can't—"

"She can and she will. I know her. All she cares about is serving the High Council."

"We'll fight back. Haven't you seen our movies?"

He managed a smile. "I know humans would try. But there's no Earth-based technology that can stand up to the Coalition. No *Earth*-based technology."

"I don't understand."

"The Vegans are legends among my people. Legends because they *created* our technology. If you offer them a home here, they become your allies. They will protect the Earth—and the Coalition won't dare try anything while the Vegans have any sort of claim to it."

She took a deep breath and let it out through pursed lips. "You think I should say they can stay. As if I have that power. It's crazy."

"You have that power because they've given it to you. The Coalition has been coasting on Vegan technology that was given to us thousands of years ago. Imagine what the original inventors have accomplished in that time."

A horrible thought coalesced in his mind. The Tau Ceti's technological level had just jumped well past that of the Coalition's. No one knew how they had managed it.

But if they'd had help… If there were Vegans who had changed their basic philosophy and were determined to find a new homeworld at any cost—moons, if the legends about them were just plain wrong—there would be no force in the galaxy that could stop them.

Sarah pulled him from his dark thoughts, reaching out and trailing her fingertips along his cheek. "I'll do it. I'm trusting you, Ari."

"I know."

He leaned down to kiss her. The act felt as natural as breathing. She melted against him, her arms winding around his neck, drawing him closer.

What started as reassurance turned to something more. Heat, passion, a connection unlike any he had ever known. If the Vegans hadn't been waiting for them, he was sure they would have ended up back upstairs. But the Vegans *were* waiting.

They broke off the kiss, but kept their bodies close, arms wrapped around each other.

"I'm ready," she called.

# Chapter Twelve

Despite what she said, Sarah was not ready for this. She was *so* not ready. But Ari was with her, and that made it a little better.

Cerulean appeared in the windowsill, and then hopped down to the floor. He had been completely invisible a moment before. Cyan and Violet shimmered into view behind him.

"You can become invisible," she said.

He cocked his head to the side. "Of course. All Vegans have personal cloaking devices as part of our exo-suits."

*Exo-suits. Right.*

Ari had not exaggerated about their technology. She was sure of it. Not only because she'd just seen it in action, but because Cerulean was so chill about it. She could easily imagine him finishing his comment with, "Can't *everyone* become invisible at will?"

This was going to work. It had to.

"I would like to officially welcome you to Earth," she said. "On the condition that you work with me and...the First Contact committee."

Stars, was she really saying this?

She turned to Ari. "What did they call themselves?"

"The Department of Homeworld Security."

That name made more sense now.

"Right," she said. "Them."

Violet looked very nearly as angry as it seemed possible for a lizard to look. Her lips were curled down in a deep frown, the purple of her stripes had darkened till they looked like bruises, and the fringe around her neck and head quivered in what Sarah was pretty sure was barely suppressed rage.

Somehow, that made Sarah feel better about the whole thing.

Cerulean bowed low. "We are honored to accept your invitation and terms. Please allow us to return the gesture of hospitality by welcoming you to our society, finalizing our alliance."

"Welcoming...how?"

"We invite you to the Life Ship for a special ceremony and festival, marking the partnership of our two species."

"I...um..." She glanced up at Ari, who nodded encouragement. "I accept."

"This is ridiculous," Violet yelled. "We do not need to bind ourselves to this inferior species."

Cerulean and even Cyan turned and hissed at her, their language changing to pops, clicks, and sibilance.

Violet backed away from them. "You do not speak for

all of us."

She leapt onto the windowsill, then disappeared.

"Okay. That was disturbing," Sarah said.

Cerulean shook his head. His frills slowly flattened against his neck again. "Violet and a few others have different ideas about how our society should advance. Luckily, they are a very small minority."

"That's not very reassuring." Especially since Violet had gone so far as to scare Sarah out of the tree.

*Holy crap, Violet actually* has *been trying to kill me.*

"Once the ceremony is over and you are officially a Vegan, there will be no turning from this path and unity will be restored," Cyan said.

"The sooner the better, then." Sarah really hoped Cyan was right.

"We can depart immediately." Cerulean headed for the door to the dining area. "We have a cloaked vessel just outside."

"Sarah, wait." Ari grabbed Sarah's hand. "Accept me as your bondmate."

"What?"

Bondmate… That sounded a lot like being married.

"They won't let me go with you if we aren't bonded."

Cerulean turned toward them and cocked his head to the side. "The Sadirian is correct. We assumed due to your mating ritual that you were already a bonded pair."

Sarah felt her cheeks heat. "You weren't watching us,

were you?"

"Of course not." Cerulean actually might have turned a bit greener. Was it possible for a reptile to look nauseated? "You were quite loud, however."

Cyan nodded. "We had to create a noise dampening field around the treehouse for our own peace of mind."

"Oh." Sarah's cheeks heated even more. "But if I invite him to the Life Ship, surely—"

"Only Vegans are permitted aboard. You, as Protector, are considered Vegan even though we have not completed the official ceremony. Your bondmate would also be granted this status." Cerulean stared at her, as if willing her to pick up on some concealed message.

It wasn't hidden that well anyway.

Bondmates. As if this day couldn't get weirder or more intense.

She looked over at Ari, who wore the sweetest expression—hovering between anticipation and nervousness.

If things between them had been allowed to progress naturally, she couldn't say they wouldn't be in this position eventually. She couldn't even say she hadn't already thought about it. But this was making it a reality. Really, really fast.

Then again, her reality had become pretty damned weird in the last couple of hours.

The idea of going with the Vegans to their Life Ship by

herself was frightening. Especially knowing that Violet wasn't the only one who had it in for Sarah. She needed backup. She needed support. She needed Ari.

She *wanted* Ari.

"Ari is my bondmate," she said.

He let out a breath and closed his eyes briefly. When he opened them, he cast one of those brilliant, heart-stopping smiles at her. He picked her up and hugged her, burying his face in the side of her neck.

As he set her on her feet, he whispered, "Bondmate."

He brushed her hair away from her face. Then he kissed her.

It was slow and deep, his tongue sliding between her lips and dancing with hers as if they'd been kissing like this forever. As if they *would* kiss like this forever.

She hoped so.

"Excuse me." Cerulean had tilted his head back and was grimacing. "The ship is ready."

Apparently, kissing wasn't something the Vegans were used to witnessing. With their lizard lips, she didn't know how they would kiss if they tried. How did Vegans show affection?

Her display with Ari seemed not to sit well with Cerulean. Which made it all the more meaningful to Sarah.

The kiss had nothing to do with his mission or the Vegans or their situation. It was only Ari and Sarah. Wanting each other. Caring for each other. It was about possibilities far removed from what they were dealing with. Possibilities she couldn't wait to explore.

"We have made an official record of your union." Cyan ran her hand along the silver band that ran down her arm. She looked like she was grinning.

"Okay, then," Sarah said. "Let's go."

# Chapter Thirteen

The mission had definitely taken an unexpected turn. Ari was in a cloaked Vegan vessel and sitting next to an Earthling he had spent an incredible night with—and was now pair-bonded to.

He couldn't even say he had any regrets. Whatever happened going forward he would face with Sarah. They would help Earth through the challenges ahead. With the Vegans on their side, they actually stood a chance.

The ship they were riding in helped his optimism. It was incredible.

Instead of close spaces and chrome, with views of the outside primarily serving the pilots, they were in a round... sitting room. That's what Brendan would call it.

The bottom of the ship was white and the entire top half was some transparent material. The pilots—two Vegans that Sarah had apparently not met yet—rested on what looked like branches growing out of the ship's floor and trained to reach their control consoles. The Vegans were able to maneuver the ship by passing their hands over the panels in front of them. They didn't even have to touch anything.

A ring of cushioned seating framed the back half of the ship, forming a semi-circle. Sarah was at his side, holding his hand while she chatted with Cyan. Cerulean silently watched from across the cozy space.

"Your curiosity is obvious, Sadirian," Cerulean said.

Ari bowed his head. "Forgive me. This vessel is unlike anything I've ever seen."

"There is no forgiveness necessary for curiosity." The Vegan's lips pulled up on one side in something like a smirk. "Curiosity is the forerunner to advancement. Do you have any questions?"

Ari couldn't let such an opportunity pass by. "The ship is so spacious. Was it designed with Earthlings in mind?"

Cyan laughed. "Sadirians focus too much on physical efficiency. We recognize that sentient beings have spiritual needs as well."

How did a larger space meet spiritual needs? Ari wasn't even sure what that meant.

Now that he thought about it, the ship *did* remind him of the space beneath Sarah's treehouse. She'd explained to him that it was meant to be a place that soothed people's emotions and minds. He felt a similar sense of serenity in both locations.

"Does the design make you uncomfortable?" Cyan asked.

"I guess I'm accustomed to the tighter quarters aboard

our ships," Ari said.

"Is that how you were able to get around in my treehouse so well?" Sarah cocked her head so she could look at him. The gesture seemed oddly Vegan.

"Yes," he said. "It's actually the most comfortable dwelling I've encountered on Earth."

"I'm glad you like it so well. I'm hoping you'll be spending a lot more time there." She grinned at him, but then her eyes widened suddenly and she crawled onto his lap.

It would have been more enjoyable if she'd been looking at him, but she was staring out the window at something over his shoulder instead. He turned in his seat so that he could see what had caught her attention and his heart started to pound.

*The Life Ship.*

It rested on the deep blue waters of Earth's oceans. Uncloaked.

"I see the fear on your face, Sadirian," Cerulean said. "The Life Ship is only visible through the viewports of this vessel. The cloaking systems are on the same frequency."

"How do you manage that?" Ari said.

The Vegan smirked again. "We have advanced our cloaking mechanisms quite a bit since we last interacted with Sadirians."

Ari held Sarah against his chest as they watched their vessel descend toward the enormous Life Ship. It must be miles across, made up of circular sub-levels connected through various walkways.

Everything was covered in green. Colorful buildings rose up around trees and grass interspersed with colorful plant life. It looked like an island, except for its perfectly circular shape.

How did the ship maintain its structural integrity while traveling through space? How did the Vegans protect the life on the surface when there was no apparent dome or structure covering it?

"It's beautiful," Sarah breathed.

It was. And he'd once again fallen into the Sadirian mindset of looking at its physical efficiencies.

"It's a miracle," he said.

She smiled at him, picking up his hand and squeezing it tight.

They landed on a circular pad that pulsed with a soft blue light. Sarah didn't hesitate when the hatch opened. She boldly followed Cerulean, and Ari followed her.

They walked down a broad staircase, to the edge of a humongous field of low grass filled with Vegans. There must be thousands present. Tens of thousands, even.

Sarah did pause then.

Ari wrapped his arm around her, offering his support. The landing they were standing on was high enough that the gathered Vegans could see. They all looked about the same size as Cerulean and his friends.

Cerulean started to speak in their Vegan language. The crowd seemed rapt as his speech built in intensity. Finally, they began to cheer, waving their short arms in the air and leaping up and down.

Cerulean gestured for Sarah to step forward. She didn't glance back at Ari. Instead, she just stiffened her spine and joined Cerulean on the edge of the dais.

Ari's heart seemed to grow as warmth flooded his chest. Her courage amazed him even more than the Life Ship. The Vegans had chosen their Protector well.

Another Vegan, one Ari hadn't seen before, stepped forward holding a tray with two thick bands of silver on it. Sarah looked to Cerulean for guidance. He took the bands from the tray and turned to her.

"Earthling-Vegan Sarah, do you accept the role of Protector—granting permission for us to moor the Life Ship on your oceans, to assist in the healing of your world, and to work with us for the betterment of both our peoples?"

"Sounds good to me," she said. She smiled at Ari, her cheeks flushed. "I mean, I accept."

"Hold out your arms, please," Cerulean said.

She did, and Cerulean stepped forward, holding the bands underneath her wrists. They started vibrating, then sprang apart briefly before snapping onto Sarah's wrists and rejoining in seamless circles.

She stepped back in surprise, looking at the thick

wristbands. "Um, what's happening?"

"All Vegans wear exo-suits to interact with our environments," Cerulean said. "We began work on yours some time ago. Our engineers will immediately begin creating one for your bondmate."

Ari was going to get an exo-suit? He suddenly understood the Earth gesture of the fist-pump that he sometimes saw Brendan and Henry make while playing video games.

"How is this an exo-suit?" Sarah asked.

Cerulean grinned. "Give it a moment."

The wristbands started to glow. Metal unfolded from them, trailing up along her arms. Ari could see it moving down her spine under her dress before it appeared on her legs, wrapping thin, evenly spaced bands around them as well.

The bands became thinner as more silvery substance swept up and over her head, until she was wearing a gleaming suit of...incredibly sexy mech-armor. The metal looked almost like jewelry—a perfect balance of sleek metal and smooth skin.

The faceplate framing her face looked distinctly reptilian and the suit even had a tail. It dragged behind her, though, unlike the actual tails of the Vegans.

Aside from the artistry that made the suit beautiful to look at, the technology was incredible. Ari could only imagine all of the things such a suit would be able to do.

"Due to your physiological differences, the tail will take some time to adjust to," Cerulean said. "Eventually, you will learn to control everything. The suit will respond to your thoughts. It will react as if it is part of you."

Sarah turned in a slow circle with her arms spread wide, watching her tail drag behind her. "This is either intensely cool or intensely terrifying. I haven't figured out which, yet."

"Give it time. Soon—"

Cerulean's words were cut off as another vessel shot past them. Ari grabbed Sarah, trying to wrap his body around hers to keep her safe. In her new exo-suit, he found he couldn't budge her.

A group of Vegans scattered as the ship landed in front of them. Others remained close.

The hatch opened, and three Vegans filed out. The first was Violet.

"Seriously?" Sarah said. "Come on, Violet. We're on the same side, now."

"Not yet," Violet said. "The ceremony is not complete until you demonstrate full integration with your exo-suit. If you can't control it, you can't protect us."

"Okay, well, give me a minute."

"I claim the right of challenge," Violet said.

The Vegans on the dais gasped. Cyan covered her mouth with her fingertips.

"Violet, I beg you not to do this," Cerulean said.

"I am within my rights to do so. I challenge the Earthling Sarah for the rank of Protector. It has not yet been decided."

"I don't understand," Sarah said. "I thought I was already the Protector."

"Violet is right." Cerulean turned a deeper shade of green. "Until you have demonstrated control of your exo-suit, you will not officially be considered a Vegan. We were prepared to guide you through this during the ceremony."

"And she can just interrupt?"

"Any Vegan can challenge the candidate when a new Protector is chosen," Violet shouted.

"We haven't selected a Protector in centuries," Cyan said. "Violet is taking advantage of outdated laws."

"But *laws*, nonetheless." Cerulean turned to Sarah and sighed. "You don't have to do this. If you forfeit, we will take you back to your treehouse and leave you in peace."

And if she did, Earth wouldn't just be facing the threat of the Coalition. Ari was certain that Violet and her group had plans for the planet as well. If Violet took over as Protector, she would start with Earth and then expand from there. Ari wasn't certain she and her group weren't already colluding with other sentients. The entire galaxy was at risk.

"Is this like a duel or something?" Sarah asked.

Ari hadn't encountered that word yet, and his cultural indoctrination session hadn't covered it. "What's a duel?"

"Where two people fight for a common prize or to redeem their honor or something," Sarah said.

"It is like that." Cerulean nodded gravely.

"Who chooses the weapons?" Sarah said.

Violet sneered at her. "There are no weapons. Just our exo-suits."

Ari couldn't believe that Sarah was considering going forward with this, even with everything that was at stake. If something happened to her...

He couldn't face that possibility.

He stepped forward, and said, "I'll do it."

"No," Violet said. "The challenge has been issued to Sarah and only she may accept or decline."

Ari's stomach twisted. "Sarah, please. You don't know what you're getting into."

"Yeah, I've been hearing that a lot lately. But look at where 'getting into stuff' has gotten me. I'm on an alien vessel in the middle of the ocean, surrounded by new life forms. And I'm with you."

"But—"

She stood on tiptoe so she could reach out and press a finger to his lips briefly. "It's my turn to ask you to trust me."

# Chapter Fourteen

Sarah could do this. She was sure of it.

Mostly sure.

Somewhat.

"The challenge will commence now," Cerulean said.

"What, like 'now' now?" Sarah asked.

Violet hissed and sprang at Sarah. Reflexively, she leapt out of the way.

Leapt fifty feet out of the way. The exo-suit didn't just respond to her thoughts—it increased her strength and speed, apparently.

"Shit shit shit shit shit!" Sarah yelled.

The Vegans beneath her scattered as she landed. She was able to roll to absorb some of the shock. Her exo-suit took the brunt of it, but it still felt like she'd rattled some teeth loose. She kept her inertia going, rising up onto her feet just like back in her gymnast days. The tail made it a bit awkward, but she still kept her balance.

*How did I do that?*

Cerulean had said the suit responded to her thoughts. All the years of training—even so long ago—had trained her muscle memory. Her mind and body remembered what it was like, even if she hadn't kept up her practice. And she *had* been doing plenty of mind-body integration exercises lately, like yoga.

Whatever was helping her out, she was grateful, because when she turned around Violet was right behind her.

Sarah tried to punt her opponent, but Violet darted out of the way. This could get old fast. Especially if Violet intended to just wear Sarah down.

"I don't understand why you're doing this, Violet." Sarah dodged again, this time controlling her ascent more carefully and landing without the jarring impact.

"I don't expect you to understand." Violet said. "You're an unevolved creature with a miniscule intellect."

"I hope you're as bad at fighting as you are at insulting people."

Violet planted her feet and bowed her head. At first, Sarah thought she might be relenting. Then Violet's exo-suit began to glow.

The metal fanned out, expanding in size while retaining the same shape until the armor was a little over five feet tall. The Vegan remained in the center of it, operating the exo-suit's limbs as if they were her own.

"You look surprised, Earthling," Violet said. "Did you not consider that we would develop technologies to let us operate in environments made for sentients of varying size?"

Sarah hadn't had a chance to consider much of anything. Except the driving belief behind everything she was doing.

"I still believe we can peacefully coexist," Sarah said.

"Why peacefully coexist when we could easily rule?"

Violet swung around in a circle, lashing out with her tail faster than Sarah could react. She'd been too focused on Violet's arms and legs. Sarah fell to the ground, scrambling to get back to her feet, but wasn't fast enough.

Violet was on her in an instant. She lifted Sarah from the ground and held her in the air. Sarah could feel pressure on her exo-suit. It was starting to register as pain. Sparks sprayed out as Violet's metal claws dug into Sarah's suit.

She should have seen the tail coming. Violet was a lizard-person. A Vegan.

But now, so was Sarah.

Clearing her mind, she imagined her energy flowing down through the tail of her exo-suit, like she imagined her energy flowing through her own body in yoga. The tail twitched once, then lashed out and smacked Violet in the face. Well, smacked her ex-suit in the face.

It was enough of a surprise to get Violet to drop Sarah. She pressed her advantage immediately, leaping forward and catching Violet somewhere near her suit's "ribs" and lifting her from the ground.

Violet bit down on the back of Sarah's exo-suit. If Sarah had the same ridge of spines that ran down the Vegan's bodies, that would have really hurt.

But she didn't.

Just as Sarah had been thinking too much like an Earthling, Violet was thinking like a Vegan. And her arms and legs were much shorter than a human's.

Sarah struck Violet's faceplate with her elbow, rolling her opponent off of her. Violet landed in a crouch, then immediately sprang forward again. Sarah was ready.

When Violet was within range—an instant before she realized it, thanks to Sarah's longer arms—Sarah punched Violet in the side of the head. The blow sent her reeling, small arms flailing as she tried to regain her balance.

Sarah kicked Violet's exo-suit in the leg, then wrapped her arms around the neck of the mechanical armor. Violet's actual body was safely several inches below, so Sarah didn't hold back. She lifted the suit, squeezing the vulnerable spot as hard as she could.

Her own exo-suit responded to her thoughts perfectly— even memories of wrestling moves she'd seen on TV as a kid. Sarah stepped on Violet's tail to keep it pinned.

Violet's suit twitched a few times, but no matter what Violet tried, she couldn't get purchase to free herself. With Sarah's grip on Violet's neck, her tail immobilized, and her limbs too short to reach anything vital, Sarah had won.

"Yield," Sarah said.

"Never."

All Sarah had available was the tail of her exo-suit. Very carefully, she imagined it rising and snaking through the rib pieces of Violet's exo-suit. She watched it closely, stopping it just short of piercing the Vegan's scaled skin. The tip looked sharp and deadly.

"Yield." Sarah did her best to sound menacing, even though there was no way she would actually hurt Violet.

Violet didn't have to know that.

"I...yield."

Sarah didn't trust Violet enough to let her go. It wasn't until Cerulean spoke that Sarah knew it was over.

"The challenge is complete," Cerulean said. "The Earthling-Vegan Sarah has earned the rank of Protector."

The Vegans cheered even louder than before.

Sarah lowered Violet to the ground, watching in awe as her exo-suit shrank back to normal proportions and seemed to meld with her scaled skin.

"You showed me mercy," Violet said. "Others will take advantage of that. How will you be able to protect us if you can't even kill our enemies?"

"Are you my enemy, Violet?" Sarah asked.

Violet didn't answer. Sarah stepped closer and said, "You underestimated me because I'm not one of you. And I kicked your ass because of it. What makes you think the Coalition will fare any better against us?"

The corner of Violet's mouth twitched up in a smile. It didn't last long. Her expression returned to its usual grimace.

Violet bowed deeply and said, "Protector."

# Chapter Fifteen

"Let me get this straight." Ari's commanding officer, Kira, rubbed a spot between her eyebrows. Her bondmate, Brendan, sat next to her at one of the tables in The Old Oak, his eyebrows hiked up his forehead as he also tried to process everything.

Ari gave Kira a moment to collect her thoughts. He had given her a great deal of data in a short amount of time.

She took a deep breath, and said, "The source of the anomalous readings was a sentient species that you believe to be the Vegans—and they claim they have permission from an Earthling to be on the planet."

"And this Earthling has formed an alliance with them," Brendan added.

Ari shook his head. "It's more than an alliance. They now consider themselves both Earthlings and Vegans."

"And so does the human?" Kira said.

Ari nodded. "She's been integrated into their society."

"Is there anything more I should know about?"

"Um..." Ari wasn't sure how to explain the rest. Especially about him and Sarah.

Sarah walked out of the kitchen of The Old Oak carrying a tray with five glasses filled with green liquid. Cerulean was sitting on one of her shoulders, perched more like a bird than a lizard. He was chittering and clicking. Sarah nodded in response.

After the ceremony and festivities, Sarah had insisted they start teaching her how to speak in the Vegan language. Ari planned to learn it, too.

Cerulean smiled at them. "Ah, this is your Sadirian planetary liaison."

Kira's frown deepened. "You are the alien lifeform claiming to be from Vega."

"Claiming?" Cerulean clicked something at Sarah and she laughed.

"Wherever they were from originally, they're part of Earth now." Sarah set the drinks down in front of each person at the table

The confidence in her tone was well deserved after how well she'd adapted to the exo-suit. Its silver bands had melded onto her skin, looking like ornate jewelry around her neck, arms, legs, and...other places that he had carefully inspected. To make sure she was comfortable.

Ari had helped her train a few times and couldn't wait to receive his own. He'd be even better able to help her, the Vegans, and Earth afterwards. To help everyone in the Coalition.

"That's not your call," Kira said.

"Isn't it?" Sarah said. "Who gets to decide then? You?"

Kira's deep voice remained level. "The situation is complicated."

"Complicated." Sarah pursed her lips and nodded. "I suppose it's a good thing we have a First Contact committee to sort things out."

Kira glared at Ari.

Brendan leaned over and said, "I think you mean 'Department of Homeworld Security'."

Kira turned her glare at him.

"We know about the Sadirian vessel on its way to Earth," Sarah said. "With the help of the Vegans, Earth will be in a much better negotiating position. The Coalition won't dare make a move to piss us off."

"Except it isn't all of Earth that has the Vegans," Kira said. "It's you. One Earthling living in a...treehouse."

"One Earthling and my Sadirian bondmate."

"*Bondmate?*" Kira closed her eyes, rubbing her temples. "That isn't on record."

"Actually, it is part of the Vegan archives," Cerulean said. "Which I believe you will find are recognized by the High Council."

"If you actually *are* Vegans," Kira said. "I'm not convinced."

Cerulean cocked his head at her. "You think it such an impossible chance to have encountered us again in the vastness of this universe. I say that it is much less probable that I should meet you—an awakened Sadirian."

Kira stiffened. "Awakened?"

"It is our term for one who was born with the innate gift of controlling our technology with the mind alone," Cerulean said. "Very rare among Vegans. Unheard of in any other species."

"I don't know what you're talking about," Kira said.

Cerulean laughed. "You have nanites living within your brain. They are a fundamental part of Vegan technology. I can hear them through my exo-suit. *You* can hear them without one."

She and Brendan exchanged a glance.

Ari was too stunned to say anything. He knew the Coalition had installed a nanNet in Kira's brain—something usually done to improve the functionality of citizens that were considered to be sub-standard in performance. It would give her better recall and increase her mental acuity. He'd never heard of anyone being able to talk to the nanites, though.

"How the hell do you know that?" Brendan asked.

Cerulean shrugged. "They told me."

"Okay," Kira said. "I'm a little more convinced."

Brendan steepled his fingers and leaned back in his chair. "First order of business—I think we should invite Sarah to join the Department of Homeworld Security. We've been working on recruiting more representatives. I'll contact the others as soon as possible and make sure they're in agreement."

"I think the second order of business should be to reassign me to the Vegans," Ari said. He wasn't sure what "order of business" meant, but it sounded official.

Kira nodded. "Agreed."

"And the third order of business…" Sarah lifted her glass high above the table. "A toast to Earth's future. May our friendships help the world—or galaxy, I guess—become a better place for everyone."

"Indeed." Cerulean jumped to the table and picked up his Vegan-sized glass.

"I can drink to that." Brendan eyed the contents skeptically and shrugged. "I hope."

Ari lifted his drink and tapped it to Sarah's, sharing the toast—which he'd learned simply meant sipping the delightful beverage after a brief statement from one of the people participating in the toast—and was not at all related to heated bread.

Brendan grimaced and set the glass back down. "Ugh, that is disgusting. I think it just added five years to my life, though. Is there kale in that? You health nuts always put kale in things."

Sarah grinned at him. "That would be telling."

Brendan smiled back. "Did you guys really pair-bond within less than forty-eight hours of meeting?"

"We did." Sarah leaned into Ari and he wrapped his arm around her shoulders.

"That is a story I have to hear." Brendan reached for Kira's hand and interlaced their fingers without seeming to think about the act. Kira's lips twitched up in a smile.

Ari could feel his own smile all the way to his toes. His heart felt light and full at the same time. Endless possibilities had opened up to him. All because of Sarah.

"Well, it started with these lizards…" she said.

# Epilogue

"What do you mean you can't trade with me anymore?" Carol tapped her pencil against the smooth surface of her desk with increasing speed. The graphite broke.

"Please understand, Dr. Addison." Craig's voice crackled on her phone, some new interference entering their conversation—probably since he was calling her on a different channel than normal. "Barbara and I are working with the Department of Homeworld Security now. We can't jeopardize Earth's chance of forming a first contact committee by continuing our smuggling operations. The safety of your planet is at stake."

"I need *you* to understand. This is a matter of life and death."

She shouldn't have let that slip out. And yet, the little gasp she heard Craig let out gave her a glimmer of hope.

*Please, please, please, give me what I need.*

"If it's that important..." he began.

Her heart seemed to be stuck in her throat during his long pause.

"You should approach the Department for help," Craig

said.

Her voice seemed clogged with all the possible words she could use to try to tell him he was wrong, that he needed to help her, even if she couldn't explain. If she shared too much, she would cause more harm than good.

"They're very helpful people," Craig said.

"Every other time you've mentioned Sadirians, you warned me to never trust them."

"Well, yes, but these Sadirians aren't like the others we've encountered. And they're working with some very friendly humans. If you can explain what you need those particular chemicals for—"

"I can't."

Craig and Barbara, she barely trusted. These others were complete unknowns. Carol couldn't risk it. She'd find another way.

"Thank you for your assistance," she said.

She ended the call, then slammed both hands on her desk with enough force that her pencil snapped in half. She dropped the pieces and dusted off her hands. After a few deep breaths, she started to sort through the data that she had about her situation.

By her calculations, she had enough serum on hand to last another month. Barely. She would find another supplier. She had time.

*Right, a few weeks is enough time to make contact with another alien smuggler who can provide me with chemicals that aren't found on Earth and won't ask for anything in trade that will harm my planet or other sentients—or ask too many questions.*

Craig and Barbara had only asked for various seeds and small amounts of soil samples. It had been easy to provide, especially after they'd told her they would be using them to assist with recovering other planets' compromised ecosystems. She'd worked with the Lyrians long enough to trust them—for over twenty-five years.

*Ever since he was born...*

She pulled out her phone and dialed the first number on her recent call list. When it went to voicemail, she wasn't surprised. It was the middle of the workday for people with regular jobs.

As soon as she heard the beep, she said, "Kyle, it's your mother. Call me as soon as you get this." She hung up and set the phone on the table.

She couldn't run out of serum. She would find a way to get what she needed.

Too much was at stake for her to fail.

—

The Vegans aren't the only "little green men" (and women) running around on Earth. Our next couple are about to get the surprise of their lives! And then things *really* get complicated. Read on for a sneak peek at *Invasive Species.*

# Invasive Species

## The Department of Homeworld Security
## Book Eight

## Chapter One

"This was a mistake."

The bartended pointed at the beer in front of Kyle. "That's the drink you ordered, buddy."

"No, I was talking to myself," Kyle said.

The bartender shrugged and walked away.

"And now I really am talking to myself."

Kyle looked over at the group of friends who had insisted he join them on their trip to the bar. Supposedly, Mitch was feeling down after his most recent breakup and needed moral support. Watching him chat up every woman who passed his table made Kyle wonder if that had been a ruse. Mitch had once said, "The more beefcake in the window, the more customers stop by to shop."

Kyle picked up his drink and turned toward the mass of people dancing or playing pool or just trying to get from one place to the other in the packed room. His skin was crawling.

Mitch wasn't exaggerating about Kyle's beefcake status. Navigating the thick group was going to be a pain in the ass just from his sheer size. The messenger's bag Kyle always carried would only make things worse. It wouldn't be easy to avoid bumping into people with the narrow spaces they were leaving between each other.

He watched the patterns of movement in the crowd, weaving in and out among them with only minor jostling and quite a few muttered apologies until he reached a corner that was a little quieter than the rest of the place. A couch filled the area, with a low coffee table in front of it.

Unfortunately, the couch wasn't empty. An auburn-haired woman looked up at him from the book she was reading.

He looked at the cover—a sleek spacecraft on a star field with two familiar characters' faces superimposed in front of it all. Maybe *not* "unfortunately".

"Hi," he said.

"Hi." She smiled, her amber-brown eyes crinkling a little as if she really meant it.

He glanced around, not really sure what to say. "I don't mean to interrupt. If you're at a really good part, I can go."

"A really good part?"

He gestured toward the book. "You're going old-school. It's a special experience."

She laughed. "True. But I hate to send you back into that morass of humanity after you fought so hard to escape."

"I appreciate your compassion." As soon as he could, he would head home for some peace and quiet.

After he talked to the intriguing redhead.

"How can you read with all this noise and…chaos?" he asked.

"I have seven younger brothers and sisters. You learn."

"Wow, I can't even imagine." When she arched an eyebrow at him, he added, "Only child."

"There were days I dreamt of that. Not many, though. My siblings are cool."

He looked around at the empty seats, and said, "Are any of them here with you?"

"No, I'm with…" She looked around, then sat up a little straighter. "Hang on."

Kyle caught a glimpse of a dragon on the bookmark she tucked into her book before setting it on the table. She pulled out her phone and read something that made her let out a little snort.

"Apparently, I'm with a bunch of bailers who left an hour ago and didn't bother to tell me because 'I was busy reading'." She picked her book up again and leaned back. "If they wanted me to pay attention to them, they shouldn't have scheduled this outing on a release day."

Kyle scoffed. "I'm missing book club for this."

That same eyebrow arched on her forehead as she looked him up and down. He let out a sigh.

"No, I wasn't the High School quarterback, and yes, I do love to read. This ridiculous growth spurt," he gestured to his torso, "happened in college. It's genetic—according to my mother, the PhD in genetics—and it drives me crazy."

"How you must suffer from your amazing physique and Hollywood hero good-looks."

He tried to ignore the sparks that crackled down his spine at her words. "Amazing, huh?"

She let out another snorting laugh. "This is a really bad pick-up ploy."

"I just wanted to get away from the crowd. When I came over here, I couldn't even see you. I wasn't trying to pick you up."

"Sure."

"But after talking to you…"

She smirked. "My mastery of sarcasm and choice in mentally stimulating pastimes has captured your interest?"

"That and your choice in authors. I set my alarm for midnight so I could wake up and read that book as soon as it downloaded."

This time, she all-out laughed. "You read Scifi

Romance?"

"I call it 'space opera' to avoid annoying conversations. And I read everything." He waved his hand toward her book, and said, "Don't think I didn't notice that High Fantasy style bookmark you're using. I know another genre-hopper when I see one."

Her eyes narrowed as she seemed to look at him for the first time. At his *face*, mostly, which was a relief.

"The only reason I'm here is because I already finished it," he said. "I had to see how the author resolved the plotline with the missing space station and find out whether Daphne and Boreal would find each other again."

"But it wasn't resolved. They found the space station, but Daphne wasn't there."

He lifted his glass. "And that is why this beverage has alcohol in it. It's going to feel like a long wait for the next book."

She laughed again, but the edge to it was gone. Then she scooted over on the couch.

"Thanks." He sat next to her, and said, "I'm Kyle, by the way."

"Tracey."

He leaned forward to look at her book again. "If you're only half-way through the book, how do you know about the space station? We didn't see what happened to it till close to the end."

"Second read-through. You weren't the only one up at

midnight reading a digital copy. Then I ran to my favorite bookstore as soon as it opened to get a paper version."

"That is dedication."

"Yeah. I bet you read yours on your phone at the gym."

He pulled off his bag and set it on the table, then reached inside and pulled out his pristine print copy of the book. "I was saving it to read tonight, but my friends dragged me here."

"What's that?" She pointed at the table.

His heart seemed to stutter, then started pounding. "That's my autoinjector."

He grabbed it, then turned it over in his hands, making sure it hadn't been damaged when it rolled out of his bag. He couldn't believe he hadn't even noticed it. There were about seven hours till he needed his next dose, but after the last time he'd been late… He never wanted to go through that agony again.

"You allergic to peanuts or something?" she said.

Kyle placed the injector back in his bag and made sure it was sealed tight. "More like the planet. Ever read H.G. Wells' *War of the Worlds?*"

"Yikes. You seem a lot nicer than those invading Martians."

"Thanks." He let the word drip with sarcasm, since it seemed to be her native language.

"On behalf of Earth, we welcome you," she said. "And your allergies. As long as you're not, you know. Trying to take over the planet."

"That isn't on my agenda for tonight." He leaned back against the couch, grinning at her as their banter put him at ease.

A super-cute bookworm who knew classic Scifi as well as modern. He might not be after the planet, but he was seriously interested in the "Earthling" in front of him. This was the most fun he'd ever had flirting. How long could they keep up the jokes about him being an alien?

*'I wish,'* he thought. *'It would explain a lot.'*

"Next time you're sucked into an outing on a release day, you should download the audio version," she said. "You can enjoy your book with headphones while you pretend you're drinking and listening to the conversation."

It took him a minute to remember what they'd been talking about. When he did, he sat back, struck by how much more tolerable that would make gatherings like this in the future. "That is a great idea. I can't believe I never thought of it."

"Like I said, lots of siblings. You come up with coping mechanisms."

"When I came over here, I didn't mean to interrupt your reading. But…"

"But now that we're talking…" She leaned forward, resting her elbows on her knees. "You don't really want to stop."

"Yeah."

"Me either."

He didn't try to mask his grin as he held up his copy of the book. "I'm glad we're on the same page."

—

# About the Author

USA Today Bestselling author Cassandra Chandler uses her vivid imagination to make the world more interesting, spawning the ideas she turns into her whimsical Science Fiction romcoms and darkly evocative Paranormal and Urban Fantasy Romances. Fast-paced and funny, lighthearted or dark, her stories will introduce you to characters you want to be friends with and worlds where you'd like to build a vacation home.

www.ingramcontent.com/pod-product-compliance
Lightning Source LLC
Chambersburg PA
CBHW051252170626
46809CB00004B/1613